The Amazing Master Daviel Amberstcrombie

The Mystery of the Stolen Daggers

Book 2

Daniel S. Wyckoff, Sr.

Candle in the Window

THE MYSTERY OF THE STOLEN DAGGERS

This book is a work of fiction. All characters, events, and settings are products of the author's imagination. Any resemblance of any person, living or dead, events, or settings is purely coincidental or used fictitiously.

Paperback ISBN: 978-1-7346566-8-8

Ebook ISBN: 978-1-7346566-9-5

All Scripture is taken from the King James Bible.

This book is rated PG

Contents

1. THE BOY'S SURPRISES — 1

2. SETTLING IN AT LAST — 7

3. MANROVIA ROYALTY — 21

4. LETI AND DREW VISIT — 34

5. OPEN HOUSE — 50

6. STOLEN DAGGERS — 65

7. A TRIP TO MEXICO — 84

8. THE WYCKOFF FAMILY — 102

9. SAND MOUNTAIN CAVE — 109

10. ESCAPE — 121

11. GOING HOME — 129

12. KIDNAPPED — 135

13. HAL TO THE RESCUE — 149

14. THE CHASE — 159

15. THE VICTORY CELEBRATION — 166

Sneak Peek — 175

Also by Daniel S. Wyckoff, Sr. 185

The Adventures Contiune... 187

CHAPTER 1
THE BOY'S SURPRISES

Daviel (Dah-V-El) had bought himself an island with a large mansion on it and with a mystery to solve. The mystery was solved in Book 1 "THE MYSTERY OF CRESCENT HOOK ISLAND but not before Daviel and Hal were captured and tied up and the treasure stolen. While he and his best friend Hal were solving the mystery, Daviel did not have time to explore the island and settle into his new home. To find out about the hidden stairway, secret staircases in the mansion, and the cave, you must read Book 1.

His "mom" was helping him with buying furniture and decorating. Daviel, an orphan, called Mrs. McKnight his mom. Mrs. McKnight is the wife of Judge McKnight, or dad. He has lived with them for four years, since the time his parents were killed in a car accident. Mom has very good tastes and knew the value of furniture and they had a gigantic task in front of them. They had ordered bedroom furniture for the eight guest suites on the second floor. They were waiting for the furniture to arrive. The first-floor guest room was already furnished and looked great!

Daviel was very busy with fixing up the mansion. School and karate lessons would both be starting soon. After being captured in the last book, Daviel decided that he and Hal needed karate lessons.

Daviel and Hal are best friends. They have been best friends since they were thirteen. On Monday Hal turns sixteen and Daviel will be sixteen three days later.

Daviel, only five feet five and one-half inches tall, weighs one hundred twenty pounds with wavy but not curly dark red hair and green eyes. He is dark complexioned which is unusual for red heads, and has no freckles. He is a multi-millionaire worth around seventy-five million dollars and very intelligent.

Hal is black headed with blue eyes and very long eye lashes. He is five feet six inches tall and weighs one hundred thirty pounds. He is often impetuous and very good looking according to the girls. Everyone thinks he should be a movie star!

While Daviel and Hal are only best friends, they consider themselves to be brothers. Both boys live in Savannah, Georgia. Daviel will move to the island after his birthday. Hal lives on the coast and can see Daviel's island from his bedroom window.

Daviel and Hal are dedicated Christians and will attend the same Christian School and church. Daviel will live with his Aunt and Uncle who will be his cook and butler. Ed is the gardener. He and his wife Sara live in a four-bedroom house on the island close to the mansion.

The weekend passed quickly. They decided to keep the treasure a secret for a little while. Sunday night as they drove past the car dealership Hal looked for the car.

"I guess the owner finally came for his car," he said when he saw that it was not there.

"Tomorrow is your birthday. Your dad promised to take you to look at cars."

"I know," said Hal, "but I really liked that car."

Monday morning Hal's dad entered Hal's room, threw back the covers on Hal's bed and popped his son on the rear and said, "What! Are you going to spend the whole day in bed? The car dealership opens at ten so you better get moving."

"What time is it?" moaned Hal.

"It is six thirty," said his dad.

"Dad!" exclaimed Hal, "We have three and a half hours before they even open. Let me sleep."

Hal's dad laughed as he left his son's room. That was pretty fun he thought. I should do it more often. What Hal was thinking would be better kept a secret.

Daviel was an early riser so he got up, took his shower, had his devotions, and went downstairs. He was talking with Mr. Scott when Hal came down for breakfast at eight o'clock.

Daviel looked for his parents but could not find them. He figured they must have gone out to eat for breakfast. They often did that.

At ten, Daviel and Hal drove the Corvette to the car dealership. As they drove up Hal saw "his" car and a new yellow Camaro convertible sitting in the parking lot in front of the building.

Daviel pulled up next to the yellow Camaro. "Do you want to look at the Trans Am while we wait for your dad?" asked Daviel.

While the boys were looking at the T-top Firebird Trans AM and Hal was bemoaning the fact that the car was not his, his dad, mom, the Judge and Mrs. McKnight drove up in time to hear him say, "Daviel, I sure wish this car was mine. I don't think we will be able to find another one like her!"

Before Daviel could answer, John, the car salesman, came out and asked, "Would the new owner of this beautiful car like his keys?"

Hal looked to see who the new owner was. Seeing no one he looked at the man who was holding the keys out to him.

"Well, do you want them or not?" John asked with a smile.

"Me?" questioned Hal before snatching the keys out of the man's hand. He ran and gave his dad and mom a giant hug. "Did you really buy her for me?"

"No," said his dad, "Daviel did."

Hal looked at the grinning face of his best friend. "You bought me this car and you didn't tell me! You let me whine about my car being sold and you knew all along that you had bought it for me! I, I...." Hal had no words to say what he thought.

"Surprise!" yelled Daviel. "Happy Birthday"

Hal hugged his best friend as tears came to his eyes. "You are the greatest best friend in the whole world."

"Uh hum," said John looking at Hal. "I hate to interrupt but I believe there are some papers that need to be signed."

Hal and his dad went in to sign the papers. When they came back, only Daviel was still there.

"How would you like to take her for a drive?" asked his dad.

"Boy would I!" exclaimed Hal. Looking at Daviel he asked, "You're coming too, right?"

"Of course, I am, but you will have to bring me back here to get my car."

Hal looked for the Vette but could not see it.

"Not the Vette," said Daviel laughing. "This Camaro is mine. It has the same exact engine in it as yours. In fact, they are the exact same cars except yours is a Trans Am and mine is a Camaro. Remember I told you that I needed a car that I could drive every day. The Corvette is only for special occasions. Dad and mom are out driving it right now. Who knows when they will come back? You should have seen the look in dad's eyes when I gave him the keys. It was a little scary."

When the boys got back home with their cars Daviel's dad had a surprise waiting for him. In front of the house next door to Hal's house was a moving truck.

"Someone bought the house," said Daviel.

"Not someone," said his dad. "Mom and I bought it. That is our big surprise. We wanted to be closer to you so we bought the house."

Daviel jumped and shouted for joy. His mom and dad would still be close by. Could life get any better than this?

Chapter 2

Settling In At Last

Daviel moved into the mansion and his extended family all came over one morning to examine the treasure. Mr. Scott and Edward carried the heavy chest from the secret room into the library and put it on the heavy oversized oak desk that Daviel had bought. He had furnished all of the first floor except for the Home Theater/Family Room.

"I am so excited!" exclaimed Mrs. McKnight. "Just think, we are going to see a buried pirate treasure from the 1700's."

Everyone shared her excitement.

They opened the chest and separated the gold coins from the jewels. Daviel took the jeweled dagger and the jeweled crown and set them aside. As they removed the coins and jewels, they found a box. Upon opening this they found a three-string black pearl necklace.

"Oh my!" exclaimed Mrs. McKnight. "That must be worth a fortune." She held the necklace up to her throat.

"Do you like it?" asked Daviel.

"I absolutely love it," she said.

"Good, it is yours," Daviel said with a smile.

"Oh, I couldn't take this," said his mom.

"Well if you insist," said Daviel as he reached out his hand for the necklace.

As Mrs. McKnight started to hand it back with a deep longing look in her eyes Daviel said, "Keep it as an early Christmas present."

"But dear, someday you may want to give this to your wife."

"What? I do not even have a girlfriend," said Daviel blushing.

"Are you keeping secrets son?" asked his dad.

Daviel chose to ignore the comment. "You can leave it to my way future wife in your will. How does that sound?"

"Oh, thank you!" she said as she hugged him and ruffled his hair.

They continued sorting the coins and jewelry. Again, they found a box. Upon opening this they found a pair of beautiful ivory or pearl handled pistols and some shot. Hal took them and stared at them. You could tell that he really liked them.

"They are yours", said Daviel.

"I, I can't take these," said Hal.

"Why not?" asked Daviel.

The two friends argued back and forth while the adults looked on with smiles on their faces. After arguing for several minutes Daviel was getting frustrated with his friend. Finally, he grabbed him by the shirt and pulled him down the hall and into the music room.

"If I have to beat some sense into you I will," said Daviel. "By right half this treasure belongs to you and you will not take anything. Why?"

Hal remained silent.

"We are not leaving until you give me a good reason."

"Look Daviel," began Hal, "If I take these it will look bad for—"

"What do you mean look bad?" interrupted Daviel.

"I overheard some of the boys in our youth group saying that the only reason why I am your friend is because of the things you give me."

"What!" shouted Daviel. "I have not given you anything, well, not until the car, and besides who cares what someone else says. You are my best friend and I love you more than I could ever have imagined I would. You are my brother. Please Hal, I want to give them to you."

"I can't," said Hal as he started back for the library.

"Wait!" called Daviel. "How about if we ask the adults what they think – okay?"

Hal agreed to the plan. They went back to the library and they both explained their sides of the story.

Hal's dad asked, "Would you like to have those pistols son?"

"Yes sir, but...."

"Then take them," said the judge. "Never allow someone else's opinions to dictate your actions."

"That's right son. You and Daviel have been like brothers for over almost three years. Ignore what others think. You and Daviel love each other and you should not let anything or anyone come between you."

"Yeah," said Daviel. "Listen to them; I really want you to have them and whatever else you want."

Hal thought for a moment and said, "I will take the pistols, but that is it. Okay?"

"Fine," said Daviel although he was not too happy about it.

The adults had continued to sort out the treasure while the boys were "talking".

"Look what we found," said the judge holding up another dagger covered with jewels.

"It matches the other one," said Daviel excitedly.

They finally finished sorting all the treasure. "Ladies, please take some of the jewelry. I am sure there must be something you would like to have."

"Daviel, I would love this cameo broach with the diamonds around it if that would be okay," said Hal's mom.

"Please second mom, take whatever you want."

"This broach would be plenty for me son."

Daviel smiled broadly at his second mom.

"Could I have this amethyst pendant?" asked Aunt Chris.

"Would you not like the earrings that match it?" asked Daviel.

"Earrings?" questioned his aunt.

"Sure, I believe I saw a set that matched the pendant."

They all searched for the earrings and soon found them and a necklace that matched. Daviel gave them to his aunt.

"What about you Sarah, is there not anything that you would like?"

"You mean I can choose something too. I thought you only meant for your family to choose something," explained Sarah.

"You and Edward are part of my family. You two, mom and dad, Aunt Chris and Uncle Jim, and Hal's mom and dad, oh, and of course Hal, are my family. Please take whatever you want."

"Well, I did see a small emerald broach. It was in the shape of a yellow flower with the emerald in the center."

Everyone looked for the delicate piece of jewelry. Hal finally found it.

"Would you not like the necklace that matches the broach?" asked Daviel.

"Necklace," said Sarah, "I don't remember seeing a necklace."

"How about this one?" asked Daviel holding up a matching necklace. "I found it when we were looking for the broach."

"Oh, Daviel, could I have that too!"

"Of course," said Daviel and then turning to Mrs. Scott. "Would you not like something else?" he asked.

"I do like that pearl bracelet if that would be okay."

Daviel gave her the bracelet. "Ladies, if there is anything else you would like you better speak now or forever hold your peace. Mom, would you not like something that you could wear every day? Later I will have the church over for a formal dinner and you can wear the black pearls but you need something for every day. And you men, please look for something that you would like. I am sure there is something here that would suit you."

Daviel's mom and the men soon choose some jewelry.

"What about you Daviel?" asked his dad. "You have not taken anything, nor Hal."

"I have what I want," said Daviel picking up the jeweled daggers and the jeweled crown."

"I have what I want," said Hal.

Daviel frowned at his friend. Hal laughed. "Your face is going to freeze like that," joked Hal. "I think that you should hang the daggers and the crown on the stone fireplace in the theater / living room. They would look really good there."

Grabbing the daggers, crown, and Hal's hand Daviel said, "Come on" and they ran to the living room. The adults followed.

The daggers were about eighteen inches long with precious jewels covering the handles and scabbards. Everyone discussed how they could best be displayed to their best advantage on the huge stone fireplace. It was finally decided to have a box made with a glass door that would lock and hang them in it crisscrossed and the crown above them. Daviel would collect more daggers and swords to hang on the fireplace later.

They went back into the library and started putting the jewelry back into the chest. They decided to put the coins in first with the jewelry on top. As they dropped the first of the coins in the chest, the bottom sounded odd.

"Wait a minute," said Daviel. "The bottom of this chest sounds strange. Maybe there is a false bottom."

He turned over the chest and dumped out the coins then tapped on the bottom. It definitely sounded odd. Slowly he ran his hand along the bottom and sides of the trunk until he cut his hand on a piece of metal.

"Ouch!" he exclaimed pulling back his hand.

"Did you cut yourself?" asked his mom.

"Only a little," said Daviel as he went back to examining the chest. "Look! This piece sticks out."

He and the others tried to pull out the little piece but it was rusted shut.

"I will be right back," said Edward, "I have some pliers in the tool shed."

Soon he was back and they pried out the piece. As they pulled it out, the bottom section popped out. Opening it – they found a beautiful diamond necklace, choker, earrings, ring, and broach. It was absolutely gorgeous.

"Wow!" exclaimed everyone at the same time.

The diamonds sparkled in the light. There were also gemstones that looked like star sapphires and delicate tiny golden doves that hung down.

"I changed my mind," joked Mrs. Scott. "I'll take that set if you do not mind."

As Daviel stared at her she laughed. "I am only joking. What are you going to do with it?" she asked.

"I have never seen anything so beautiful," said Daviel. "I do not know what to do with it. Do you think that maybe it belonged to a princess?"

"I have an idea," said the judge. "Why don't we call the museum and see if they know of anyone who could come and look at the treasure and possibly appraise everything. I would like to know what all this is worth. It must be worth millions."

Everyone agreed to the plan so the judge called the museum. As the judge described the diamond necklace the man said that he would be right over. Thirty minutes later Mr. Brandon was standing in Daviel's library staring at the necklace.

"Well?" asked the judge.

"Where did you find this?" asked the man. No one answered.

"What can you tell us about all the treasure? We know that Captain Smythe, the pirate, buried this treasure but that is all that we know," explained the judge.

"This diamond necklace set belonged to a princess in the land of Manrovia."

"I knew it!" exclaimed Daviel interrupting Mr. Brandon.

"Her parents had it designed for her for her twenty-first birthday but as it was being delivered the ship was attacked by pirates and everyone was killed. The royal family has been searching for this for the past three hundred years. They have offered a five-million-dollar reward to whoever finds it."

"Can't Daviel keep it," asked Hal.

"Of course, he can," said Mr. Brandon. "This treasure belongs to whoever found it. Of course, the royal family of Manrovia need never know that it was found. If they knew they would want to buy it."

"You do not have to make any decision right now son. You can decide later what you want to do."

Gratefully, Daviel looked at his dad. The jewelry set was beautiful and he was not sure that he wanted to part with it.

"It will take me several hours to appraise everything here." Turning to Daviel he asked, "Do you have a pad and pen that I could list everything and their approximate values."

Daviel got the man what he wanted. He then went to work. The others went about their business but Daviel took a book from the library shelf and started to read it. Two hours later, and still on the first chapter, the man said, "You do not have to stay here and guard your treasure young man. I promise you I will not steal any of it."

Daviel looked at the man's smiling face.

"I, I was not guarding the treasure. I just did not want to be rude and leave you all alone. I, I am sorry."

Smiling the man said, "If I were you, I would not let someone alone with this treasure either. You are wise to stay here. Your dad has been watching me from the doorway the whole time too."

Daviel looked at the doorway as his dad entered the room.

"I too apologize but we do not know you and...." He left the sentence unfinished.

"No problem," interrupted Mr. Brandon. "You are both very wise."

After three more hours had passed, he told them, "Here is a list of everything and their approximate values. I wrote down my opinions of the pieces. The pistols, that your friend has, belonged to Captain Smythe himself. He was famous for his ivory handled pistols. Everything here has an approximate value of thirteen million dollars. Of course, five million of that is the diamond necklace set."

Daviel and his dad took the list and looked at it. They saw that the black pearl necklace was worth around two-hundred fifty thousand dollars. They would not tell Mrs. McKnight.

"Do you have any plans for the treasure?" Mr. Brandon asked. "We would love to display it at the museum. We have the perfect spot for it."

"I want to talk to my dad first, but I had thought of that."

The man stood up to leave. "Please let me know what you decide to do."

"How much do I owe you," Daviel asked.

"Nothing," replied Mr. Brandon. "It was a sheer pleasure just getting to look at it. Here is my card if you decide to let us display it."

Daviel took the card and thanked him.

The judge walked out with Mr. Brandon. He had to take him back to the mainland. When he got back the others were talking about the treasure.

They put everything back into the chest and put the chest in the secret room. That night as Daviel was lying on his bed the judge came into his room to talk.

As Daviel started to get out of bed the judge said, "Stay there. I just wanted to talk for a while. Since you came to Savannah, I have not had much time to talk with you. I have missed our talks. Have you decided what to do with the treasure?"

"I think that I would like to contact the royal family of Manrovia and tell them that I have their treasures."

"That would give you another five million dollars."

"I have been thinking about that too. I do not need any more money. I have more than I need now. I think that if they are nice, I will just give them their jewels and not take the money. I would like to use this as an opportunity to witness to them."

"What if they are not kind?" asked his dad.

"I do not know. Probably I will give them the jewels anyway so that my witness will have more power."

The judge grabbed the young man in a big bear hug. "I am always so proud of you. When do you want to contact them?"

"Can we call them tomorrow? I want to call the museum and arrange for the rest of the treasure to be set up there."

"Are you giving them the treasure or just loaning it to them?

"I am just loaning it to them. I want to keep it for now. Maybe later I will donate it to the museum."

"Tell you what, I will contact my lawyer and see what we need to do. Okay."

"Thank you, dad."

They talked about other things like school, the church, Hal, girls and much more. It was getting late and Daviel was getting tired. As he was drifting off to sleep, he heard his dad say good night. The judge stood by his son's bed looking at the small young man and thinking how wonderful God was to allow Daviel to be a part of their lives.

CHAPTER 3
MANROVIA ROYALTY

Today was Saturday and the boys planned to do nothing but explore the island. They packed themselves a lunch and took bottles of water with them. If they got too hot, they could always swim in the ocean. They decided to explore the other side of the island and not the hook side. This would be the first time either of them explored there. They walked over the land in the shade of the trees. The island consisted of five hundred acres. They had a great time running here and there. It was a lot of fun but there wasn't anything exciting there to discover. They returned to the mansion in the early afternoon. They were now sitting on Daviel's bed.

"Have you heard from the king and queen of Manrovia?" asked Hal.

"Not yet, but then we only sent the message two days ago. It is not like their number is in the phone book. We sent a special courier. They should get the message sometime today."

"Do you think they will come?"

"We will have to wait and see but I would be surprised if they did not," said Daviel.

"They could always send a courier with a check to pick it up," said Hal.

"No, if it does not mean more to them than that, then I will keep it. I feel sure they will come," Daviel said.

On Monday the furniture was supposed to arrive for the upstairs suites. Last Saturday the boys had bought a surround sound home theatre system. It was five feet high by seven feet wide. There were nine different speakers and four different VCR/DVD players. The TV section sat on top of a three-foot high cabinet. It suited the room perfectly. The huge room, forty-six feet by sixty-six feet was filled with comfortable chairs and tables. Daviel's two jeweled handled daggers were proudly displayed on the fireplace along with the jewel studded crown. Later he would look for more daggers and swords.

"Let's go and watch a movie on your new theater system," suggested Hal.

"Sure!" said Daviel. "We have a couple of hours before dinner. How about if we go for a ride in the

Corvette tonight? I love to ride in her at night with the top down. You can drive."

"You bet!" exclaimed Hal. He loved to drive the fully restored 1976 Corvette convertible.

After dinner the phone rang. "Hello," said Daviel, "Oh hello dad. What is up?"

"I just got a call from the Queen of Manrovia. They will be here next Friday. I told them that you would put them up at the mansion. There will be the King, Queen, their fourteen-year old son, and three servants. I figure they could all stay in the left wing."

"Great dad, I hope the furniture arrives soon. I do not think that the King and Queen would like sleeping on the floor."

Laughing the judge said, "It's okay. The furniture people called and said they would deliver all the furniture on Monday. That will give us a few days to get organized."

"Thanks dad. Hal and I are going for a ride in the Vette later. We should be home by nine-thirty or ten."

"Have fun and drive carefully."

"We always do. Tell mom I love her and we will see you tomorrow at church. Good night."

After hanging up Hal asked, "What's up?"

"The King and Queen of Manrovia are coming on Friday with their fourteen-year old son. All the second–floor furniture will definitely be here on Monday so we will have a few days to get everything set up."

"Do we have to carry everything up those stairs?" asked Hal.

Laughing Daviel said, "No, I hired some men to do that. All they have to do is put the furniture in the right colored room. Mom had a great idea when we painted all the rooms a different color. I wonder if the King and Queen sleep in the same quarters."

On Monday the barge was ready to bring over the furniture. As the trucks drove up the neighbors came out to see what they could. All the furniture was of the best quality and cost Daviel a small fortune. It was also very heavy. Daviel was glad for the helpers he had hired. It took all day but everything was placed in its proper room. Tomorrow they would start arranging everything. Daviel ordered pizzas for all the helpers. After eating, the hired workers went home.

"That was a big job," said Mrs. McKnight. "I sure am glad you hired all those strong men."

"Me too mom, however; we will be plenty busy setting up all the rooms tomorrow," said Daviel.

"It will probably take us a couple of days. Did you see how the colors all blended together? They will be beautiful suites," mom said.

Everyone went to bed early. Daviel's mom and dad spent the night in the downstairs guest suite. Hal's parents said that they would return the next day.

Bright and early Aunt Chris fixed everyone breakfast – her famous Belgium Waffles. While she and Sarah washed the dishes Daviel, mom, dad, Hal, Mr. & Mrs. Scott, Edward, and Uncle Jim went to work. Mom had Daviel make sketches of all the rooms so everyone knew where everything was to be placed. Also, all the rooms were going to be set up the exact same way so that made things a little easier.

They finished unpacking everything and got it all set up in one day. They were standing back admiring the different rooms when a phone rang.

"Hello," said the judge. He listened and interjected a few comments here and there. When he hung up, he said, "The Queen and her son will be here Wednesday. The King will follow on Friday. It seems the queen could not wait to see the family heirlooms."

"At least the rooms are ready for them," said Mrs. McKnight.

"When will they arrive?" asked Daviel. "I sure am glad that the rooms are ready!"

"Their plane lands at two. I will pick them up and bring them here. Oh, yeah, they also will be bringing three security men."

"Great," Daviel said but not too enthusiastically.

Wednesday morning Aunt Chris and Sarah went shopping for food. They figured the royal family would stay until Monday. Daviel hoped that they would not be a royal pain.

At three, the judge pulled up to the island's dock beside Daviel's beautiful yacht. The queen and prince exited first. She was very pretty and the prince was handsome. He looked about twelve.

"Welcome to my home," said Daviel as he kissed the queen's hand. "I am sorry that your husband, the king, could not make it at this time. I trust that your flight was a good one."

Laughing the queen said, "Please, kind sir, you need not be so formal. My name is Mia and this is my son Jeremy. Please call us by our names."

"My name is Daviel and this is my mom, Mrs. McKnight and this is my best friend Hal; you have already met my dad."

Everyone greeted one another. "May we help with your bags?" asked Hal.

"Oh no, we have servants for that. Actually, we traveled fairly light. We only have two bags apiece. If you would be so kind as to show us to our rooms, I would appreciate it."

"Certainly, your majesty. Fo —"

"It's Mia," interrupted the queen.

"Oh, sorry, ma'am. Follow me. I have put you in the left-wing suites. Will your husband share your suite or will he require one of his own?"

"He will stay with me thank you. By the way, how old are you?"

"I am sixteen. I hope you will enjoy your stay. Jeremy, do you like to swim?"

"Oh, yes, do you have a pool?"

"No, I have something much better! I have a hidden cove that is very private. Maybe we could go there tomorrow. Hal and I swim there often."

The queen and Jeremy got settled into their rooms. The queen assigned rooms to her staff and helpers. It was nice to have guests at the mansion. As they came down Aunt Chris asked if anyone would care for some refreshments. There were finger sandwiches and pastries.

"Shall I serve in the formal dining room or the normal one Daviel?"

"How about we use the formal one? I have been dying for a chance to use it. After refreshments I will give you a tour of the mansion and then I suppose you would like to see the necklace and other pieces of jewelry."

"Yes, I am so excited. My family has been searching for it for over three hundred years."

After refreshments and the tour, they all went to the formal sitting room. Daviel excused himself to get the necklace from his room. He had put the jewelry in the safe in his room so that he would not have to show anyone where the secret room was. Upon returning, Daviel handed the box of jewels to the queen. Everyone sat back looking at her face as she opened the box.

"Wow!" exclaimed Jeremy.

The queen stared in awe at the beautiful jewelry. She then held the necklace up to her throat.

"May I help you put it on?" asked Daviel. "There is a mirror over there."

After putting on the necklace the queen walked over to the mirror. The sight of the necklace took her breath away. Quietly she returned to her seat, took off the necklace and started to hand the box back to Daviel.

"You may keep them your majesty," said Daviel. "I am curious about something though, what do the little gold doves mean."

"I am the first in my family to wear this beautiful necklace. I am speechless. I am surprised that you did not keep it," said the queen.

"To be honest, I thought about it but after I learned their history, I felt that they should be returned to their rightful owners," explained Daviel.

"Thank you Master Daviel. Words cannot express my gratitude. The doves represent the Holy Spirit. My great, great, great, who knows how many greats, grandmother was a Christian and her parents designed the necklace to reflect her commitment to Christ."

"I knew it!" exclaimed Daviel. "And you, are you a Christian too?"

"Oh yes, as are my husband and Jeremy. We come from a long line of believers' in our Lord. Are you a Christian too?"

"Every one of us in this room has put their faith and trust in Jesus Christ for our salvation. We are all happy to hear you have done the same," said the judge.

"I knew there was something about all of you when we first met. I thought you might be Christians. I was going to work it into the conversation but Daviel beat me to it."

"He can be very abrupt at times. I am glad that he did not offend you," said Hal.

"Oh no, I like men who speak their mind. That way I know where they stand."

"You always know where Daviel stands; on everything," said Hal teasingly.

"What about you, young man."

"Me!" squeaked Hal. "Yes, ma'am, I always try to be honest and –"

Daviel interrupted. "You will find Mia that Hal is loyal and always honest."

They talked about other things and soon the judge could see that their guests were getting tired.

"Daviel why don't you show your guests to their quarters? It has been a long day for them," said the judge.

"I am sorry. I should have thought of that. Please feel free to go to bed. I think I will have a little snack before retiring. How about you Hal, Jeremy?"

"I think I will just go to bed if that is all right. I am tired," said Jeremy.

"Good night all, breakfast is at eight o'clock if that is okay with your majesty," said Aunt Chris.

"That will be fine."

As the queen and the prince were heading up the stairs, they could hear Aunt Chris yelling for the boys not to mess up her clean kitchen.

The next day and a half passed quickly. Soon the king would arrive. Daviel, Hal, and Jeremy had a great time swimming at the hook. Jeremy was having a wonderful time. Normally he was closely guarded but here on the island he had a lot more freedom. No one knew the royal family was there.

At three o'clock the judge arrived with the king. He was by himself, no security guards. After everyone was introduced the queen took the king to their suite. They stayed there talking for a couple of hours and came down for dinner. They had turkey with dressing and all the trimmings. The food as always was delicious. After dinner, coffee, pie and homemade ice-cream were served. Even Daviel and Hal were full afterwards.

"Why don't we all go to the theatre / family room. The chairs there are quite comfortable," suggested Mrs. McKnight.

Everyone found comfortable chairs and sat down to talk. While they were talking the king said, "Daviel, the queen tells me that you are only sixteen years old. I am curious and do not mean to offend but how did you come to be so rich?"

"I inherited the money when I was thirteen from a man whose life my biological father saved. My biological parents were killed in a car accident short-ly before my thirteenth birthday. After some hard lessons and a lot of love and help from mom and dad McKnight, I learned how to handle the money. Hal has been the greatest best friend. He never asks for money and I have to force him to take whatever I want to buy him. He can be a real pain in the rear sometimes, but I guess I will keep him. Good friends are hard to come by."

Hal had a shocked look on his face and everyone laughed.

"How did you come to buy this island and where did you find the treasure?" asked the king.

Daviel and Hal related all the events that led up to their finding the treasure. (If you want to know what happened you will have to read book 1).

"That was quite a story," said the king as he pulled something out of his coat pocket handing it to Daviel. "Here is the reward money. The Bank of Manrovia will pay you the five million dollars reward."

Daviel took the check. "This really belongs to Hal. He actually found the treasure."

Daviel tried to hand the check to Hal but he would not take it. The judge was ready to say 'Now don't start that again boys' when Daviel said, "Thank you sir but I do not want the reward. If Hal will not take it then you may keep the money."

Daviel tore up the check and handed it back to the king. "I already have more money than I know what to do with. Why do you not use the money to help your people? I am sure there must be some- one in your country who could use some financial help."

"You are a remarkable young man. I do not know of another person in the world who would refuse five million dollars no matter how wealthy he was."

"Thank you, sir, but the credit goes to my mom and dad and especially the Lord. The necklace belongs to you and I am simply returning it."

"Well," said the judge. "I guess that clears everything up. How about if we watch something on Daviel's surround sound theater system? I have been wanting to try it out."

They spent a very enjoyable evening watching movies and munching on snacks. When it was time to go to bed the king said, "I do not remember when I have been able to relax like I did tonight." Looking at his wife he said, "Sweetheart, I think we should plan a vacation here soon, just so we can relax, that is if Daviel does not mind."

"Please come and visit anytime you wish. My island is secluded and it is a great place to relax. I would love to have you all visit again."

It was late when everyone went to bed. On Sunday everyone went to church and on Monday the Judge drove everyone to the airport. After the goodbyes were said Daviel headed to his new home to relax. Sitting in his living room looking at the jeweled daggers he sighed. It was great to be home and settled in.

CHAPTER 4
LETI AND DREW VISIT

It was the weekend and Daviel was lying in bed being lazy. Hal and his family were gone for the weekend and Daviel had no plans. After not appearing for breakfast, his uncle poked his head into Daviel's room.

"Sorry to disturb you, but your aunt and I were concerned that you might be ill."

"I am sorry Uncle Jim; I was just being lazy. I may stay in bed all day," Daviel said smiling and stretching in his bed.

Smiling at the boy, Daviel was sixteen but would always be a boy to his uncle. Jim said, "Would you like brunch in bed?"

"How late is it?" asked Daviel.

"It is ten thirty."

"My, I have been lazy this morning. Could I really have brunch in bed?" he asked sheepishly.

Uncle Jim said that he could and went to find his wife to prepare something for the boy. Twenty minutes later he was back with a tray full of food.

"I cannot eat all of that!" exclaimed Daviel looking at the tray.

"Your aunt was not sure if you would like a breakfast brunch or a lunch brunch so she sent both. What you do not eat now you can have later."

"I think I would like the sandwich and coffee cake. The rest you can take back. Thank you, Uncle Jim."

Daviel ate and thought about what he might like to do. I could go swimming, or I could take out the Vette or the Camaro, or I could take out the yacht, or I could do one hundred other things. He decided to take a shower while he pondered about the day. As he was getting out of the shower the phone rang. It was the curator at the museum.

"I am sorry to disturb you but I was wondering if today would be a good day to come for Captain Smythe's treasure, that is if you still want to loan it to us. We have the perfect display set up for it."

"Please forgive me, I have been so busy buying furniture and arranging everything how I wanted it, that I forgot to call. Please come by today. Oh, you will need to bring some strong men to carry it. Do you want me to meet you at my boat dock or do you want to come to the island?"

"I think it would be best if we came to the island. Our security men are going to help bring it to the museum. We are all very excited about being able to display the treasure. Please accept our thanks. Will two o'clock be a good time for us to come?"

"That would be great. I will see you then. Good-bye. Uncle Jim!" yelled Daviel as he ran out of his bedroom in his underwear. Luckily, he remembered he was not dressed before he left his private quarters or Shirley, the young lady cleaning the downstairs hallway, would have gotten a big surprise. Quickly returning to his bedroom Daviel threw on some clothes and went looking for his uncle. He found him in the kitchen talking with his wife.

"So, you finally decided to get out of bed," said his aunt.

"Yes ma'am. I forgot my tray but I will get it in a minute. Uncle Jim, do you think that you, Edward, and I could get the treasure out of the secret room and into the library?"

"I am sure we could. Why?"

"The museum called. Mr. Brandon said that they would like to come for it at two o'clock. I need it out of the secret room before then. And besides that, I thought I would like to look through it again before it went to the museum in case there was anything in there I might want."

"I will go and get Edward. We will be right there."

Daviel went to the library after taking his aunt his tray. Soon Edward and his uncle came. They managed to get the heavy chest onto the floor beside Daviel's desk. Daviel spent the next hour and a half looking at the treasure. He took out some of the jewels and set them aside. He would decide how he wanted them set later. He knew the judge would like some new cufflinks. He also thought that some of the stones would make nice rings. He set aside some small dainty stones and small diamonds to be made into a bracelet for a girl that he had his eye on. He was working up the nerve to ask her out. Even his best friend Hal did not know how he felt about her. At least he thought he did not. This was one closely guarded secret. Rita, thought Daviel with a smile. He was still daydreaming when his uncle entered the room and cleared his throat. "Uh hum."

"Oh, sorry, I was just daydreaming," said Daviel. He could feel his face turning red.

"And what is her name?" teased his uncle.

"That is a secret that I think even Hal does not know and he knows everything there is to know about me."

"I see," said his uncle smiling. His nephew was indeed growing up. "The museum men are at the dock."

Daviel led the men into the library. There Mr. Brandon signed the agreement that Daviel's attorney had drawn up. Daviel gave Mr. Brandon a copy and kept a copy for himself. He also gave Mr. Brandon a copy of the list of the treasure that he was sending to the museum. That way they both would know what was sent.

"We will be having a grand opening of the display on Friday. Can you be there?" asked Mr. Brandon.

"Yes sir, I will be there."

Daviel was glad to get the treasure out of the mansion. Even though no one knew about the treasure or the secret room he did not want to take any chances. Now everyone would enjoy the treasure.

Friday came and Daviel, his mom and dad, Hal and his family went to the museum to see the exhibit. Everything was beautifully displayed and labeled. Daviel and Hal were excited to read all about the treasure and Captain Smythe.

"When Drew and Leti come next week, we have to bring them to see this exhibit," said Daviel.

"Drew will love having a pirate for his ancestor," said Hal.

On Friday many people came out to see the grand opening of the exhibit and several asked the boys where they found the treasure. They said that that information would remain a secret. After seeing the display, they all went out for ice cream and then went to their homes.

Leti, Drew, and Bobby arrived on Monday. Daviel picked them up in his yacht because he wanted to impress them. After hugs of greetings Drew asked, "Where is your island?"

"Do you see that big island right out there? That is it."

"Wow!" said Drew and Bobby.

"If you will follow me, we will get on my new yacht and ride over to the island," said Daviel pointing to his beautiful yacht.

Daviel's yacht is a one hundred forty-two feet by thirty-six feet yacht with a lower deck, main deck, upper deck, and sky lounge and pilot house. It is a Saint Jamison yacht with four passenger cabins that can sleep eight or more, two crew cabins that can sleep four and a captain's cabin. There is also an owner's suite and elevator. She can cruise at 25 knots and go 6000 nautical miles. She is a 2001 model and cost Daviel six and a half million dollars but Daviel loves her. The interior of the yacht is very elegant. It has a wooden spiral stairway from the main deck to the upper deck.

The lower deck consists of the captain's cabin, crew cabins, VIP suite, engine room and exercise room. The galley is on the main deck. The main deck also consists of the dining room, living room, sun bathing deck, swimming deck, restrooms, and more. There is also a Jacuzzi in the sun–bathing area. The upper deck consists of two VIP suites, pilot house and the owners suite with private deck. Above the top deck is the sky lounge. All the rooms are beautifully decorated. In fact, the whole yacht is very elegant.

"That is yours?" asked Drew.

"Yes, it is. Are you all ready? Aunt Chris has lunch waiting for us so we better get moving."

Hal helped Leti onto the yacht as the other boys carried the luggage. Leti had parked her car in the Scott's garage. They were quiet on the ride to the island. Daviel's guests were trying to take in all the sights.

As they prepared to dock Hal said, "If you look up there you can see the mansion. Daviel and his mom have done a wonderful job furnishing it. It is absolutely beautiful. In fact, this weekend, Daviel has invited the church and some neighborhood friends over for an open house."

"I figured," said Daviel, "that you all could help me entertain everyone. It will be an open house so people will come, have some refreshments, tour the mansion, and then leave. I figure that by Friday you boys should be able to help with the tours."

"Great!" exclaimed Bobby. "Do we get to see the secret room?"

"Hal and I decided to let you boys try and find the entrances yourself, but if you have not found them by Thursday morning, we will show them to you. We have found two entrances but I suspect there are more. I have been too busy to look."

"Maybe we will find some that you haven't," said Drew. "This is going to be fun."

Uncle Jim and Aunt Chris, Edward and Sarah met them at the dock. Uncle Jim took Leti's arm and helped her climb the hill up to the mansion. Everyone else helped with the luggage.

"My, My!" exclaimed Leti. "The video that you sent us did not do justice to your home. She is beautiful. Daviel you need some rocking chairs on the front porch. I bet you get a nice breeze here at night."

"That is a good idea. Tomorrow we will go and buy some."

Daviel gathered everyone in front of the double front doors. "Okay, you three close your eyes until I open the doors. I will tell you when to open them." Opening the double doors, he said, "Open your eyes."

His friends looked into the mansion. They stood on the front porch looking in with their mouths open.

"Do not just stand there, come on in."

He grabbed Leti's arm and ushered her into the magnificent foyer. Drew and Bobby did not need a second invitation. They ran in and looked all around.

The others carried in the luggage and set it in the foyer.

"Daviel can show you the mansion after lunch. It is ready and I don't want it to get cold," said Aunt Chris as she ushered everyone into the everyday dining room. They had a wonderful meal as Daviel's guests praised the mansion.

"You haven't seen anything yet. The foyer is impressive but wait until you see the rest of the place," explained Hal.

After lunch Daviel gave them the grand tour. He put Leti in the downstairs guest room so she would not have to go up and down the stairs. He gave the boys the option of staying in one of the guest suites or staying in his rooms with him. They chose to stay with him.

Sitting in the theater/family room Leti exclaimed, "Daviel, it is so beautiful. You and your mom have decorated everything so nicely. Whose idea was the different colored guest suites?"

"That was mom's idea. I really like it. I can say Uncle Jim take the luggage to the blue room or the pink room and he knows exactly where to go, not that we have had any guests except for the King, Queen, and Prince of Manrovia."

"What!" shouted Drew. "You didn't tell us about that."

The rest of the day was spent settling in and explaining about the treasure, the heirlooms, and the King and Queens visit. After Dinner they retired to the theatre / family room to watch some videos. At ten Leti said that she was tired and retired to her suite. The four boys went to Daviel's rooms so as not to disturb her.

They talked long into the night. Drew and Bobby planned on exploring the mansion for the secret passages in the morning.

After searching for a few hours and after lunch they decided to go to the hidden cove and go swimming. Daviel took one of his boats into the cove since he did not want to show them where the secret passages were until they had a couple days to search.

The four boys had a great time swimming in the cove. They laid on the giant rock sunning themselves, talking, and drying in the sun. Finally, they got dressed and went back to the mansion. Drew and Bobby searched some more while Daviel talked with Leti. They made plans to go to the museum the next day.

Everyone awoke early and after breakfast Daviel drove his Camaro to the museum.

The museum was three stories high. It used to be the Baptist College and was built in the early nineteen-hundreds. It was completely updated a few years ago. The city was worried about the old wiring catching on fire and the old plumbing bursting and destroying some of the valuable treasure inside. The security system was also updated.

The boys and grandma entered the beautiful old building and looked at several of the exhibits. The first-floor exhibits contained memorabilia on the history of Savannah and the Smythe treasure that Daviel wanted Drew to see. The second-floor exhibits consisted of memorabilia from the civil war and other antiques from that period of time. The top-floor exhibits contained antique jewelry from ancient history and miscellaneous antique objects from around the world.

"The exhibit that I want you to see is through that door," said Daviel pointing to the door in front of them.

"What's so special about this exhibit?" asked Bobby.

"It is something special that I want Drew to see. Come on!"

After entering the room, Daviel and Hal noticed the museum had added a life size picture of Captain Smythe.

"That's new," said Hal pointing to the picture. "I wonder where they found it?"

"We found it," said Mr. Brandon, "in an old book at the library. We had this one made up so that we could display it here."

As the boys and Leti were reading about the Pirate Captain someone said, "That boy there looks like the old pirate," and pointed at Drew.

"Yes, he does," said someone else.

"Well look at that," said another person, "you could be his ancestor."

"Now you know why I wanted you to see this exhibit. Captain Smythe may just be Drew's ancestor."

"What is your name boy?" asked a man.

"It's, it's Drew, Drew Smythe."

"Well what do you know? I bet that old pirate was an ancestor of yours. You sure do look like him. Hey Mr. Brandon, if this boy is the great–great whatever grandson of Captain Smythe would the treasure that Daviel found belong to him?"

Mr. Brandon turned to Daviel and said, "No, the statute of limitations ran out on this treasure many, many years ago so Daviel is the owner. However, if Daviel wanted to give the treasure to the pirate's ancestor that would have to be his choice."

"What about it Daviel, are you going to give this boy the treasure," a man asked with a laugh.

"It just so happens that Drew is a very good friend of mine and yes if he can prove that he is the heir of Captain Smythe I would share the treasure with him because he is my adopted brother. I would not share it with any of his other ancestors though."

Daviel said that to keep anyone from getting the idea into their head about claiming the treasure by saying they were an ancestor of the old pirate. They looked at the exhibit and examined others and finally went home.

"Could I talk to you and grandma?" asked Daviel.

"Sure," said Drew. The others started to leave.

"You do not have to go," said Daviel. "I do not mind if you hear what I have to say."

They all went into Daviel's bedroom's sitting area where they would have some privacy.

"Drew," began Daviel, "I had planned on this being a surprise but after today I think we should talk. I have always planned on giving you some money on your eighteenth birthday. If you can prove you are an ancestor of the old pirate you can have the treasure or I will keep it and give you the money that I planned to give you on your birthday which is more than the treasure is worth."

"You don't have to give me anything. You already paid three million dollars ransom for me and I do not want your money."

"I got that money back. When we captured Alan and told the police our story the court gave me the money back with interest. You are like a kid brother to me and I have always planned on giving you some money. I just want to wait to give it to you when I know that you can handle being a millionaire. I plan to do the same for Hal though I suspect he will not want it."

"You got that right!" exclaimed Hal.

"We will discuss that later. Grandma, I would like to know if Drew is an ancestor of Captain Smythe, not because of the treasure but because of my curiosity. Do you have any information?"

"I do believe that my husband traced his family tree back to the sixteen-hundreds. I have a copy of it somewhere at the house. I will look for it when we get home."

"Good!" exclaimed Daviel.

"Daviel, just how much money are you planning on giving me?" asked Drew.

"My plans are to give you ten million dollars after taxes on your eighteenth birthday but that would depend on you. If you grow up to be a rogue, I shall not give you anything, but if you grow up to be a godly young man then the ten million is yours."

"Wow!" exclaimed Drew and Bobby together.

"How many millions do you have now?" asked Bobby.

"Around seventy-five million more or less but that is a secret. Why?"

"I was wondering if you wanted to adopt another little brother?" asked Bobby.

Everyone laughed. That night Hal talked to Daviel as they lay in bed.

"I think you made one young boy very happy today," said Hal.

"I would like to make another young man very happy too," said Daviel looking at his friend.

"You already have. Just being your best friend and brother makes me the happiest young man in the whole world. I do not want your money Daviel. I never have."

"I know that Hal. You have been and are the greatest best friend that a man could want."

"What is this man business? All I see is a boy," laughed Hal.

"Boy is it. I will show you who the boy is and who the man is here."

He started tickling his friend who started tickling Daviel. They were making so much noise that Drew and Bobby ran into the room and got into the act. After they stopped with everyone's sides hurting from being tickled Drew asked, "What brought that on?"

"We were just horsing around," Daviel explained. "I hope we did not wake you boys up."

"No sir, old man," mocked Drew. "We were getting ready for bed and talking. I guess we will go back to our room. Good night."

Daviel thought about showing his kid brother who the old man was but decided it was late and they needed to go to bed.

Hal and Daviel continued to talk for a while. Soon they were both fast asleep. Tomorrow was the big day. It would be Daviel's open house for the church and selected friends in the community. It would be a very busy day.

CHAPTER 5
OPEN HOUSE

It was a beautiful morning. Daviel had hired a crew of boats to transport people back and forth from the island. All of his family was there along with Hal's parents. Edward and Sarah would bring the guests to the porch where they could sit in the rocking chairs while waiting for their turn to come into the mansion. They would be giving tours to groups of ten. The four boys were going to give the tours while Daviel's servants stood on guard to see that nothing was stolen. The ladies, Aunt Chris, Mrs. Scott, and Leti would be serving refreshments in the formal dining room and cleaning up. The judge and Mr. Scott would walk around so that their presence would deter any thefts as Daviel had purchased many different and valuable knickknacks. The first visitors were due to arrive at ten. It was now five minutes to ten.

"Well everyone, today is the big day. I appreciate all of your help. Let us get to our stations," said Daviel.

The first group of neighbors arrived at ten-o-five and were taken on a tour by Hal. While they were eating refreshments the second tour was given by Drew. For the next two hours they had a steady group of people who came. It was now time for lunch. The tours would resume again at one and close at four. Everyone, including the hired boat workers, came to the mansion for lunch. During lunch they discussed any problems that they had seen and worked out solutions.

"I think," said the judge, "that our biggest groups will come between one thirty and four. I am surprised that we have not seen very many people from church."

His prediction turned out to be prophetic. All four tours had to be given one after another and still people were sitting on the porch in the rocking chairs.

As Daviel's group was being served refreshments Daviel told his grandmother, "Your idea about the rocking chairs was wonderful. Everyone seems to be enjoying them today."

Smiling, grandma patted his arm and continued with her work. They were kept busy until four o'clock. The last tour group was finishing their refreshments. As they were leaving the pastor and some church members showed up.

"I am sorry Daviel but we had car problems and only just now got here. If you do not want to give us a tour, we will come back another day."

Daviel was tempted to accept the offer until he noticed that Rita was in the group. He quickly changed his mind. "Oh, no, pastor, I am sure that Hal would be glad to give you all the tour and we still have plenty of refreshments. Go on in."

As the group passed, Daviel took Rita's arm. "How would you like a private tour?" he whispered.

Rita was very flattered. She and Daviel had been talking lately and Daviel's mom and dad were very happy about it. As Daviel and Rita walked off by themselves the judge said to his wife, "Our son is growing up. I like Rita. What do you think?"

"I think that our son has very good taste in young ladies," she said as she went back to the kitchen.

After everyone had left Daviel took a lot of good-natured teasing. The day had been a success. Everyone was tired and went to bed early. As Daviel lay in bed he was thinking. He was glad that Hal went to sleep quickly for once. He lay in his bed thinking about Rita. Her parents had given permission for her to go on the yacht ride with them tomorrow. Daviel had a surprise for Hal. Pam, the girl Hal liked was coming too. He could not wait to see his brothers face tomorrow.

After breakfast Daviel and Hal drove to Rita's house. Daviel took a lot of ribbing from his friend. If Hal only knew the surprise waiting for him!

"Why do you not wait in the car while I go and get Rita," suggested Daviel.

"Okay lover boy."

Smiling to himself, remembering Hal's comment, Daviel knocked on Rita's door. She was waiting for him and let him in. After a brief talk with her parents they and Pam left. When they got to the car Hal was laying down on the back seat with his eyes closed.

Hal said without opening his eyes, "I thought you two might want to be alone. What took you so long?"

"Are you going to hog the whole back seat or do you think that you could share it?" asked Daviel.

Still with his eyes closed Hal teased, "What! Did you two have a fight already?"

"No," said Daviel, "but I think that your date would like a place to sit down."

"I do not have a date old boy. Why can't Rita sit up front with you?"

Hal was enjoying teasing his friend and was not prepared for what happened next.

"Well, I never, if you do not want to go on a date with me, Hal Scott, then you can go by yourself!" said an exasperated Pam.

Hal shot up from the back seat. "Pam!" he called excitedly. "I, I mean, I–," stammered Hal looking at his friend.

Laughingly Daviel said, "Surprise! Close your mouth boy; you are drawing flies."

Hal shut his mouth and jumped out of the convertible. He opened the door with a cheesy grin on his face. He whispered to Daviel, "I will get you for this later."

Daviel laughed and got into the car. He drove to his boat dock and then took the boat to his island. He knew a retired sea captain who was willing to pilot the yacht with his two grandsons (In their twenties) if Daviel gave them enough notice. The Captain and his two grandsons were waiting for them.

As they boarded the yacht Daviel asked, "Captain, are we the last ones to board?"

"Yes sir, shall we be off."

"By all means Captain, let us be going."

The Captain started the engines and skillfully guided the yacht into the ocean. On the trip to Devil's Cove (it would take three hours to get there) Rita, Daviel, Pam, and Hal toured the ship and talked. They were oblivious to everyone but themselves. The adults would smile whenever they passed. These were the first girls the two boys had ever shown a real interest in. Later they would be in for a lot of teasing. Drew and Bobby were busy exploring every inch of the ship. They wanted to go into the engine room but wisely Daviel had locked it.

Much quicker than the boys could have imagined they were at Devil's Cove. The captain moored the boat at one of the larger docks. Everyone on shore watched as the beautiful yacht was moored and dropped anchor. Daviel hopped out and tied her fast to the dock. The Floating Spirit, as the ship was called, glistened in the sunlight. Everyone admired her beautiful lines. They were not used to yachts of this size mooring in their harbor.

Everyone got out and walked to the restaurant. This was their first time to eat there but the restaurant had an excellent reputation. Daviel had reserved a table for the seventeen of them.

"I hope you like fish," said Daviel. At the look on Drew and Bobbies faces he laughed and said, "They have very good steaks too!"

They were all seated at their table and the waitress was taking their order. After she finished, she asked, "Who owns that beautiful yacht in the harbor?"

They told her that Daviel was the owner. The girl was impressed with him and said flirtingly, "My-oh-my, rich, young, and good looking too. Honey if you ever need a good cook for that yacht of yours, I am available," she finished with a wink and rubbed her hand along Daviel's shoulders.

Daviel was beet red but managed to answer, "Thank you ma'am, I will keep that in mind."

As the waitress left, the group laughed. Daviel's face got even redder. Turning to Rita he said, "I am sorry. That has never happened to me before. I did not know what to say."

Laughing, Rita answered, "What can I expect when I have such a handsome and rich date. I can see that I will have to guard you from the prospective females in the area."

Daviel's face got even redder if that were possible. Recovering his composure, he said, "Well thank you ma'am I would enjoy that."

It was Rita's turn to blush.

Soon the waitress returned with their food. Everyone enjoyed the meal. Drew and Bobby both got steaks and enjoyed the ribbing that they got. Daviel was on his third platter of crab legs when the waitress whispered something in his ear that made his face turn dark, dark red. As she was passing by the judge, he stopped her and whispered something to her. She did not bother Daviel after that.

Everyone except Daviel was about through eating when the waitress asked if anyone would like dessert.

The ladies all declined but the boys, except Daviel, ordered something.

"Grandma, are you going to finish those scallops?" asked Daviel.

"No dear, would you like them?"

"Yes ma'am, they can be my dessert. Besides crab legs, scallops are my favorite sea food. Thank you," said Daviel taking the scallops. There were about six of them.

"Now these are the perfect dessert. Would anyone like one?"

At the chorus of 'no thank you' he commenced to enjoy his dessert.

Finally, everyone finished. Hal asked his friend if he would like the last bite of his apple pie. "Sure!" he exclaimed. Apple pie was one of his favorite desserts.

Laughingly Rita said, "How can you eat so much and stay so skinny?"

"Normally he does not eat so much dear," said Mrs. McKnight.

"Really, I do not, but I love crab legs and besides they are mostly shells, with a little meat," Daviel said defending himself.

"I wish I could eat like that," said Pam. "I have to be careful about what I eat but Rita can eat anything she wants and never gain a pound."

"She looks good too," said Daviel before thinking about what he was saying. When everyone laughed and stared at him, he asked, "What?" When he got no answer, he thought about what had been said. Soon he started to blush.

Standing up he said, "Well now, is everyone finished?" As he walked off to pay the bill, everyone laughed. Again, his face turned red.

When he came back to the table he said, "I hope everyone enjoyed the meal. I sure did. Hal, come with me to the bathroom, okay."

"Sure," then he added, "excuse us please."

As everyone else headed for the yacht; the two friends waited in line for the bathroom. It would take a few minutes to warm up the yacht's engines.

"I sure am glad that is over," said Daviel. "I have never blushed so much in my life."

"You sure made dinner conversation interesting."

"Do you think that Rita will go out with me again?"

"Pam told me that she likes you a lot so I think she will. Oh yeah, thanks for inviting Pam."

"You bet!"

"What did the waitress whisper to you that made your face turn so red?" asked Hal.

Daviel whispered the words to Hal and Hal also blushed.

"SHE SAID THAT TO YOU!"

Daviel nodded his head yes. As the boys talked quietly about the two girls, two men were in a high-backed booth talking in Spanish, and Hal was listening. Daviel hit his friend on the arm and whispered, "It is not polite to listen to other peoples' conversations."

"Shh! I can't hear."

Daviel turned away from his friend. When they entered the bathroom, Hal grabbed Daviel's arm. "Did you hear what they were saying?"

"No, and you should not have listened either."

"They were talking about a boy with two jewel handled daggers and how they planned to steal them. They may be your daggers!"

"No way," said Daviel. "Very few people know I even have the daggers. It must be someone else's daggers. We better hurry."

After using the restroom and washing their hands the boys left. Hal purposefully walked by the booth and looked at the two men. They were Mexicans and one had a scar over his left eye. He only got a glance at the second man before Daviel pulled him away. They hurried to the yacht.After boarding, Hal talked to Daviel again. "I think that you should be very careful. Maybe you should talk to your dad about it."

"Hal, there must be thousands of other boys with daggers."

"That is true but the man specifically said jewel handled daggers. How many boys do you think would have jewel handled daggers?"

"Okay, I give up. Dad is staying with me tonight so that we can talk." At the look on Hal's face he added, "I asked him to. You know that every so often we stay up and talk. I enjoy talking with my dad and I do not get to do that much anymore so tonight we will catch up."

"Promise me that you will tell him about the men."

"I promise. It is too bad that you took music lessons instead of art lessons. You might have been able to draw a picture of the man with the scar."

"Sorry old buddy but drawing is your talent, not mine."

The ride back to the island was very pleasant. Daviel and Rita walked around the yacht talking to everyone. Sooner than they wished, they were back at the mansion.

Daviel paid the captain and his grandsons and then he and Hal took the girls back to Rita's house. Rita invited the boys in.

"I am sorry but I cannot stay. I have to get back to the island. Dad and I are supposed to have a father and son talk," explained Daviel. "Maybe we could go out for pizza Sunday night after church."

"I would like that," said Rita. "I will have to talk to my parents about it though."

"Of course!"

"Maybe we could make it a foursome," said Rita.

"That would be okay with me. How about it, would you two care to join us for pizza after church Sunday night."

Pam and Hal liked the idea. Daviel said that he would call Rita tomorrow. Both young men went home very happy boys. Hal stayed at his house and Daviel took the boat to his island. His dad was waiting for him on the front porch.

"Leti had a wonderful idea about these rocking chairs," said the judge.

Daviel sat in the one next to the judge. Quietly they rocked back and forth. They talked for a while on the porch and then went to Daviel's room. Sitting on the bed they talked about personal things like girls and what happened today including what the waitress whispered to Daviel.

"Dad, I promised Hal I would mention this to you. I do not think that there is anything to it, but Hal is worried."

"What's he worried about?"

"While we were waiting in line for the restroom, Hal heard two Mexican men making plans to steal two jewel handled daggers from some boy. I told him that it must be some other boy but he was not convinced."

"He may be right. You could be the boy they were talking about."

"But dad, very few people even know that I have the daggers."

"You forget that you had an open house yesterday and everyone saw your daggers. Those two men might have overheard someone talking about them and now plan to steal them."

"No way dad. We just traveled three hours down the coast. How could they have heard about it from someone up here?"

"Well, I don't know but it is possible." Then ruffling the boy's hair, he said, "You are probably right but it would not hurt to hide them in the secret room for a few days would it?"

"No sir. Maybe I better do it right now. They may come tonight."

After hiding the daggers in the secret room Daviel told his father good night and they went to bed.

Sunday night the boys took the girls out for pizza.

"This is much better than yesterday with everyone else all around," said Hal.

"Did you talk with your dad?"

"Yes, and we put the daggers in the secret room."

"What's that all about?" asked Pam.

The boys told them about the two men.

"Oh Daviel!" exclaimed Rita. "You will be careful."

"Of course, but I do not think that they were talking about my daggers. I only put the daggers in the secret room to please dad and Hal. In a few days I will take them back out again. Tomorrow, dad's sons and daughter will be coming for a week before going back to school. He has four grandsons who will probably stay with me. Three of them are thirteen and the oldest is fourteen. Two of the thirteen-year-olds are twins. I cannot tell them apart. They are coming tomorrow because their school starts a week before ours does."

"Dad also has around three or four other grandchildren, ten and younger, but they will stay with their parents in their suites."

After eating their pizzas, the boys took the girl's home. Hal walked Pam to her door while Daviel and Rita waited in the car. When they got to Rita's house Hal waited in the car.

That night as the boys undressed for bed Hal asked, "Did you kiss her?"

"I am not the kiss and tell type of man," responded Daviel.

"You did not kiss her either, huh. I wanted to but I thought I should wait until after a few more dates.

This dating stuff is hard. I don't know what Pam expects me to do."

"I am the first boy that Rita has ever dated and you probably are Pam's first date, and they are our first dates, so; do not worry about it."

The boys talked as they lay in bed. They both very much enjoyed their dates. They decided that they would just hold the girl's hands for a while. They knew that they needed to be careful so that their emotions would not take control over their good sense. They wanted to be godly young men and not make any mistakes. They made a promise to each other and to God that they would be virgins when they married.

Leti, Drew, and Bobby returned to their home in Columbus the next day. Daviel and Hal were sad to see them go.

CHAPTER 6
STOLEN DAGGERS

Everyone woke up early to prepare the mansion for the family. Daviel called a temp service and hired some extra help. They would come to the island each day to work and go home in time for dinner. They were being well paid. Soon the hired helpers would be arriving and they would need some instructions. Helga, the head housekeeper, would assign them their duties. Helga lived in one of the servant's suites and her two helpers lived in the other one. Daviel's aunt and uncle, who were the cook and butler, lived downstairs.

The young ladies arrived and received their instructions. Everyone was ready for the guests. Daviel took the yacht so that everyone could come to the island at one time.

The judge's family rented a fifteen-passenger bus with trailer so that they could all come together. They unloaded in the Scott's driveway and parked the bus in Daviel's garage.

"If you will pick up your luggage and follow me, I will lead you to Daviel's yacht," said the judge.

As they descended the path to the boat dock one of the boys exclaimed, "WOW!"

Everyone agreed when they saw Daviel's beautiful yacht.

Smiling, Daviel greeted everyone. "Good afternoon. Welcome aboard The Floating Spirit. I brought her so that we would not have to make more than one trip. Tomorrow we will be taking her on a long ride and spend the night on her and return the next day in time for church."

Daviel greeted everyone and when everyone was situated, he backed the yacht up and headed for the island. One of his "cousins" came to talk to him. Because he called the judge and Mrs. McKnight mom and dad, he called their children aunt and uncle making their children his cousins.

"Would you like to pilot her?" asked Daviel.

"Yes!" exclaimed Robert.

He was the oldest cousin at fourteen. Soon the three thirteen-year old cousins joined them. They too wanted to pilot but they had to wait until tomorrow. They were getting close to the island's dock so Daviel took over the wheel.

After docking everyone carried their luggage to the mansion. Everyone was impressed when they entered the beautiful foyer. Daviel took the adults and children upstairs to their suites and introduced them to their maids while Hal took the young men to Daviel's rooms and put them in two of the extra bedrooms. Everyone met downstairs.

They spent the rest of the day exploring the mansion and talking. Daviel suggested that they get a good night's sleep for tomorrow would be a big day. Daviel awoke early the next morning to check on the preparations for their voyage. The yacht had been stocked with food, sleeping bags, fishing poles and bait. Captain Beardsley and his grandsons arrived in time for breakfast. After breakfast everyone boarded the yacht. The sleeping quarters were soon filled with the adults and small children. Hal, Daviel, and the older cousins planned to sleep on deck in sleeping bags.

They planned to sail from Savannah to Charleston, spend the night on the yacht and return in the morning. All the older boys got a chance to pilot the ship. They made good time to Charleston where the ladies were put ashore to do some shopping while the men and children went fishing.

They put out to sea and agreed to return for the ladies in three hours. Daviel piloted the yacht several miles from the shore and out of the normal shipping lanes.

"We should be able to catch a good amount of fish from here," Daviel said. Then he asked, "What do you think dad?"

Daviel has never fished and wanted to be sure the place he selected was a good one. After his dad and the captain agreed with him, he lowered the yacht's anchor.

Daviel was glad that Hal, Uncle Mike, Uncle Bill, his dad, Robert and the twins were there. Also, Captain Beardsley and his grandsons were a big help. Having never fished before he had no idea what to do. The others helped the younger boys and Daviel. Everyone was having a wonderful time.

They managed to catch enough fish to cook for supper. When they picked up the ladies, they were surprised as they listened to the children tell their fishing stories.

After dinner everyone wandered around the yacht doing what they wanted. Captain Beardsley piloted the yacht around for a while and at nine dropped anchor for the night. They were far enough away so that no land was in sight. The weather forecasters promised a calm night.

Daviel and Hal each called their girls.

After talking for a little while Daviel exclaimed, "Oh my! She's beautiful!"

"You better not be talking about some other girl," said a laughing voice in his ear.

"No way!" exclaimed Daviel. "Captain Beardsley just turned on the lights for the yacht and she is beautiful, more beautiful than I had imagined she would be."

"That is better," said Rita. *"I thought that I might have some competition."*

"No one could even come close to you," said Daviel. Blushing he said, "I only have eyes for you!"

Rita gushed some unintelligible words. They talked for a little while longer and then after saying goodnight they hung up.

Everyone got ready for bed. The boys pulled on their heavier clothes. It was a little chilly in the ocean breeze. The next day after breakfast they started their return trip.

"I really enjoy being on the ocean," said his mom. "Maybe it is just being on this beautiful yacht but it has been wonderful. I slept like a baby last night."

Everyone agreed to that. They all slept well and awoke with a large appetite for breakfast.

"Wow!" exclaimed Sheri. "It is a good thing that I don't go on very many boat rides. If I ate like this every day I'd be in big trouble."

The other ladies agreed with her.

"Well Aunt Sheri," started Daviel, "if you are worried you can always run a few laps around the yacht. She is a ship not a boat by the way. That should burn off a few calories."

"Do I look like I need a diet?" she sternly asked the boy.

"Um, no ma'am but then I was not the one complaining," stated Daviel.

Everyone laughed. The trip home went well. Everyone enjoyed the smooth ride back to the island and upon arriving back at the island, carried their overnight bags to their room.

"If you have any dirty clothes that need to be washed just set them outside your door and someone will wash them and return them to your room," Daviel said.

Daviel collected all the boy's dirty clothes and took them to the laundry room because the maids did not enter his private quarters except for twice a week to clean.

During church Daviel and Hal sat with their girls during the service and talked with them afterwards. On the ride home, they took a lot of ribbing from Daviel's uncles. The boys just grinned and bare it. Actually, they enjoyed it more than they would admit.

Thursday morning the older boys spent the morning looking for the secret passage. After lunch Daviel told the boys that the entrance to the secret room could be found in the library, but he warned them not to mess up his books. After searching for a couple of hours Daviel suggested that they all go to the secret cove for a swim. Only the older boys went. They swam for a while and then lay on the big rock drying in the sun. Hal and Daviel told them about the pirate Captain Smythe and his treasure, the hidden stairs and the cave. They explained that the best way to find the cave and the stairs was by finding the secret entrance to the secret room.

When they were all dry, they got dressed and entered the boat to return to the mansion. While they were swimming the younger children had a wonderful time running around the mansion. Their mothers were getting frantic with fear that they would break something and looked quite frazzled when Daviel came back with the older boys.

"What is wrong Aunt Sheri?" asked Daviel when he saw how frazzled she looked.

"Nothing is wrong. We are wearing ourselves out following the children to be sure that they do not break something."

"Go and take a break for a while. Hal and I will entertain them with a nature walk."

Gratefully the mothers agreed.

They spent thirty minutes walking through the woods. Daviel made all the little ones hold hands. They came to a big clearing and played tag, duck-duck-goose and other games that young children like. On the way back to the mansion Daviel talked to Edward about the children cutting a bouquet of flowers for their rooms. Edward took them to the cutting garden and each child returned to the house with a large bouquet of flowers for their mommies.

They found large vases, filled them with water and placed the beautiful flowers in their rooms. After that, the children retired to the theater/family room to watch a movie before bed. After they went to bed Daviel told the older boys that he would tell them how to enter the secret room if they promised never to tell anyone the secret. They all promised. The adults followed them to the library and Daviel opened the secret panel. Everyone entered the secret room and then followed Daviel and Hal through the tunnel to the cave.

"That is where Hal and I found Captain Smythe's treasure," reported Daviel. "Tomorrow we will go to the museum and you can see the treasure. Remember, tomorrow night we are having a catered formal dinner in the dining room and ball room. I know that mom is dying to show off a certain piece of jewelry that she has."

"Does that mean that we have to dress up?" asked Shane one of the thirteen-year old twins.

"Yes, it does," replied his mother. "You and the other older boys will wear your suits."

"What are you and Hal wearing," asked Dane the other twin.

"You will have to wait until tomorrow night to find out. Oh, mom, Rita and Pam are coming to the dinner. That will be okay, right?"

"Dear," said his mom, "it is your dinner and you can invite whomever you want. It will be fun to have them here. Have you ordered corsages for the girls?"

"Yes ma'am. They told us the color of their dresses so we called the florist and ordered large wrist corsages. We will pick them up on the way to their house tomorrow. Can you and dad direct the caterers and the orchestra that is coming until I return?"

"It will be our pleasure," said the judge. "I cannot wait to see the two of you in a tux."

"We will have to leave around four to pick up our tuxes, the corsages and the girls. Will that be okay? Dinner is at six. Oh yeah, the florist should be bringing large bouquets of flowers and setting up an arch with flowers in one of the corners for pictures. I did not hire a photographer because I know that Uncle

Bill is very good with a camera." Turning to his uncle he said, "I forgot to ask you if you would mind taking pictures. Please forgive me, but would you mind?"

"I would be delighted. Besides, I brought my new camera and it will give me the perfect excuse for trying it out. I think," he said turning to everyone, "that we should take the pictures before eating."

They all thought that would be a great idea. "I will have all the pictures taken of everyone except you and your lovely dates by the time you all arrive. After I take your pictures, we will be able to eat."

"Great!" exclaimed the boys together.

They returned to the mansion and got ready for bed. Daviel and Hal were overly excited about the dinner tomorrow and could not get to sleep. They lay in bed talking. Suddenly Daviel jumped out of bed and ran to his dresser.

"What's wrong? Have you gone crazy or something?" questioned Hal while laughing.

"I forgot about these." Daviel held out his hands to show Hal the beautiful matching diamond cuff-links that he had made for him and Hal.

"These are for you. They match mine. The diamond and black onyx ones are for dad. I know that he rented a tux for the banquet. I cannot wait to see mom wearing the pearls."

They talked for a long time and finally fell asleep. Friday morning was bright and beautiful. Everyone in the mansion was invited to the banquet. Edward, Sarah, Aunt Chris, Uncle Jim and the hired workers all had the evening off. The maids would have to clean up the next day but they too would enjoy the evening. Hal's parents were coming too.

Daviel gave his dad the cufflinks first thing in the morning. His dad thanked him profusely. They went to the museum in the morning and Daviel took everyone out for lunch. Upon returning to the mansion Daviel and Hal took their showers in Daviel's large bathroom. After getting dressed they headed for Hal's house and his car. They did not drive with the T-top open because they did not want to mess up their hair. They changed into their tuxes at the store and went to the florist for the corsages. They were beautiful. They arrived at Rita's house to pick up the girls. They were a little early and had to wait a few minutes. Rita's mom took the corsages up to them. As the two girls entered the room, they took the boys breaths away. Their dresses were beautiful and the corsages matched perfectly. They both were too stunned at first to speak.

Daviel recovered first and taking Rita's hand said, "You look absolutely stunning. I like that color on you."

"Thank you, and you look very handsome in your tux."

"Thank you," he replied.

Hal and Pam exchanged similar compliments and Hal said, "Daviel, old buddy, we will have the two prettiest girls at the dinner."

"You have got that right."

The girl's parents were proud of the boy's compliments and soon pictures were being taken. Rita's mom asked her if she had her camera. Daviel had told her about the decorations and her mom wanted to be sure and have some pictures.

They left and arrived at the mansion at five-thirty. Everyone oh d and ah d over the young couples. Uncle Bill took many photos of the couples and then as a foursome and as individuals. He also took some photos of Hal with his parents.

"I will have all of these developed professionally," he declared.

"Send me the bill," said Daviel, "I will pay for all of them as my treat. I want a big one of Rita and I and another of Hal and Pam for over the fireplace or maybe in the library. Oh yeah, I also want one of mom and dad. You did take one of them together?"

"Yes, I did. I will send everyone proofs and sizes that can be ordered. How does that sound?"

"Great!" exclaimed Daviel. "Then Rita's and Pam's mothers can order what they want but remember the entire bill comes to me."

Looking around he asked, "Where is mom? I have not seen her."

"She had her picture made in secret and swore Bill to secrecy earlier. I think that she wants to make a grand entrance," said Aunt Sheri.

"Good! I cannot wait for everyone to see —"

"See what," interrupted one of the little ones.

"You will see when she comes. The decorations are beautiful and the orchestra is wonderful. I am so excited," declared Aunt Sheri.

Rita and Pam took several pictures of the decorations and of the ice statue in one corner of the dining room.

It was six fifteen when the chef announced that dinner was ready. He brought his own staff to serve and they would clean up afterwards. That was a nice surprise. After everyone was seated mom walked in wearing the black pearl necklace and earrings. Daviel had purchased the earrings to match the necklace. She was wearing a lovely white evening dress to show off the pearls.

Everyone oh d and ah d when she entered. Daviel jumped up from his chair and took her hand and kissed it. She and dad both looked elegant.

"I am sorry for making you wait but I could not help myself. I wanted to make a grand entrance."

"Mother," said Sheri, "you look absolutely stunning and where did you get those black pearls? They are gorgeous!"

"They were part of Captain Smythe's treasure and Daviel gave them to me. I only took them on the condition that he gets them back when the Lord calls me home. I felt that his wife might like them some day."

Everyone turned and looked at Rita. Daviel laughed as she blushed.

The silence that followed was broken by the head waiter. "Dinner is ready."

The dining room and ball room were beautifully decorated. The dining room table normally seated forty people. Daviel had it specially made. There were twenty-eight at the dinner so only part of the table was used. It was decorated with real silk table clothes, flowers, candles, and Daviel's best china. The ball room was set up so that the orchestra occupied one end and the ice sculpture was in one corner and the flowered arch for pictures in the other corner. There was plenty of room to move around.

The next several hours flew by. Dinner consisted of five courses. There were appetizers followed by a salad, then the steak and lobster with baked potatoes and vegetables, followed by some fruit and then dessert. All of the food was excellent. After dinner the younger children camped out in the living room and fell asleep watching videos. Some of the married couples danced to the music. The foursome strolled outside on the patio and in the gardens. While everyone danced or relaxed in the ball room the caterers cleaned up. Daviel excused himself to talk to the caterers and paid them with a large bonus.

"Thank you for a wonderful dinner. I will recommend you to everyone that I know."

"What shall I do with the extra food?" asked the head caterer.

"If you would please put it in the giant refrigerator in the kitchen, I would appreciate it. I will send some home with everyone so their families can taste your excellent cooking."

Daviel went back to the ballroom as the caterers left. At ten the orchestra packed up and left. Daviel paid them with a big bonus also. It was ten thirty. He and Hal had to get the girls back home by eleven. He took Rita, Hal, and Pam into the kitchen and they made up plates for the girl's families. They said goodnight and then left to take the girls home. They dropped Rita off first. Daviel walked her to the door. They entered the house and gave her parents the food. Her parents gave them some privacy so they could say their goodbyes. On the front porch Daviel quickly leaned over and kissed her lightly on the cheek then ran down the steps to the car.

He waved to Rita as Hal drove away. He liked having a girlfriend.

They dropped off Pam at her house. Hal walked her to the door. Her mom took the food inside and gave them a few minutes alone. Hal too gave his date a quick kiss and smiled all the way back to the car.

Both boys remained silent as they returned to the mansion. The adults were gathered in the kitchen when they came in.

"We are in here boys," called mom.

Everyone congratulated Daviel on the wonderful dinner and evening. Daviel was beaming with pride. He too had a wonderful time.

"Well boys, did you kiss them goodnight?" his dad asked with a giant smile.

They did not need to answer; their deep blushes told the whole story.

"Stop it John, you are embarrassing the boys," said Mrs. McKnight.

Everyone laughed. The two boys quietly said good-night and retired for the evening. They lay in bed on top of the covers when the judge entered. He looked down at the two young men and their smiling faces.

"I take it you both had a good time."

The boys looked at each other and their smiles turned into huge grins.

The judge ruffled the hair on both of them and left.

"Did you kiss Rita?" asked Hal.

"Did you kiss Pam?" asked Daviel.

"It was only a quick light kiss on the cheek but it was wonderful. She did not even slap me!"

"I too kissed Rita quickly on the cheek. I did not hang around to give her a chance to slap me."

The two best friends laughed as they got under the covers. They were growing up and liking it.

On Saturday they finished the left-over lobster and steak. Sunday when the boys entered their Sunday School room everyone was talking about the banquet. Rita and Pam brought their pictures. The girls ooh d and ah d over the decorations. The boys punched them in the arm and smiled. The pictures turned out well and Daviel could not wait for the professional ones to come back. His uncle said that it would take two weeks for the proofs and that he would mail them as soon as they came in. He said that he would mail Daviel a complete set of the proofs so that he and his parents could order what they wanted. That was fine with him.

Everyone went home on Monday declaring that they had a wonderful time. Daviel told them they were welcome anytime. He and Hal returned to the mansion. It was too quiet. He enjoyed the guests. The museum called and asked if he would be willing to lend the jeweled handled daggers to them for a while. He thought that if the daggers were at the museum that they would be safe there. He agreed to do it. Mr. Brandon said that he would send two security men over for them around seven in the evening. Daviel said that he would have them boxed up and ready.

At seven, the two men arrived and after signing the receipt for the daggers they left.

"Come on," said Daviel grabbing Hal's arm and running for the stairs.

Hal followed his friend to the attic and down the hall to the other end of the mansion.

"When did you get this?" asked Hal referring the high-powered telescope.

"I bought it to look at the stars and so that I could watch you in your bedroom when you were not here," joked Daviel. "Look!"

Hal looked and sure enough he could clearly see into his bedroom.

Taking back the telescope Daviel followed the security men in their boat. He gave a play by play to Hal.

"They just landed at the dock. They are getting out of the boat and walking up the dock. Wait a minute!" exclaimed Daviel.

"What?" questioned Hal.

Daviel watched as two men in stocking masks grabbed the security men knocking them out.

"Quickly Hal, call the police. Two men in stocking masks just stole my daggers."

Daviel continued to watch the two men as Hal called the police. The men, not realizing that they were being watched took off their masks. It was the two Mexican men from the restaurant and they were getting away.

Chapter 7
A Trip to Mexico

Daviel watched as the men got into a black sports car. Hal was talking to the police.

"Tell them that they just got into a black sports car and are driving away from town. I could not see the license plate."

When Hal finished talking to the police, he and Daviel ran to the boats at the island. They were going to go and check on the guards to be sure they were all right. They sped off in their boat and reached the dock at the same time as the police. The guards were just coming too.

"Are you all right?" asked the police officer.

"I am fine," said the guard. "What happened?"

Before the officer could answer the other guard came to with a moan. "Oh, my head! Where am I. Oh, I remember. Where are the daggers?"

"Stolen," said Daviel. "I saw the whole thing. The men who attacked you snuck up behind you and hit you on the head. I was watching from my mansion with my telescope."

"I am sorry," replied the security guard. "Were they insured?"

"Yes, they are, but I want them, not the money. Officer, I saw the face of both men and would like to come to police headquarters to look at some mug shots. They both were Mexicans."

"You want to come now?" asked the officer.

"Yes sir, time is of the essence if I want to recover my daggers, and I do!"

After helping the security guards to their car and checking to be sure that they were all right the boys followed the police officer to headquarters. They were taken to a room and some books of mug shots of Mexican criminals were brought to them.

They spent forty-five minutes looking at the pictures. Hal stood up to rest his eyes. Daviel was on his third book when he excitedly called out, "Officer, this is one of the men!"

"Are you sure?" asked the officer.

"Yes sir," said Daviel and then he asked Hal if he agreed.

"He is the same man that we saw in the restaurant," said Hal. "Let's keep looking for the other guy."

The officer took the picture to the Captain while the boys kept looking for the other man. Hal did not get a clear look at this man while in the restaurant but Daviel clearly saw him through the telescope.

Hal pointed to several possibilities but Daviel did not agree with him. "The man I saw has a mole just below his left eye."

"What did you say?" asked the officer.

"The man I saw has a mole just below his left eye," repeated Daviel.

"May I please see the book?" asked the officer.

Daviel gave him the book. The man turned three or four pages and asked, "Is the man in this page?"

"Yes!" exclaimed Daviel pointing to a picture.

Quickly the man took out the picture and ran to the captain's office. Soon he returned for the boys and took them to the captain.

"Are you one hundred percent sure these are the two men?" the captain asked.

"Yes sir!" Daviel said. "I saw them clearly through the telescope."

He was going to say more when a police woman entered and whispered to the captain and left.

"They found the black sports car abandoned in a back alley. They are dusting it for fingerprints. These two men are nationally known professional jewel thieves. I wonder how they knew about your daggers."

"I have no idea," replied Daviel. "It seems impossible to me that they did."

"Well, thank you boys for your help. I will get this information out at once. You may go on home. We will call you if we have any news. I will alert the highway patrols, air ports, bus stations, taxis, and all other means of transportation. We will try to keep them here in Savannah."

"Thank you, sir," said the boys as they left.

When they got to the dock, they looked around for some clues that maybe the police had missed. Hal was searching the surrounding area, including some bushes when he found a scrap of paper. Opening it he read: Hotel San Pedro, San Pedro, Coahuila. "Daviel!" he yelled, "come here, quick!"

Daviel ran to his friend. "What is it?"

"Look at this. I found a clue."

"Awesome job," he said hitting Hal on the back. "Come on, we need to show this to dad."

Running to his dad's house they knocked on Daviel's the door. It was only ten thirty so they knew they would be up.

Mrs. McKnight opened the door. "To what do we owe this unexpected pleasure?"

"Is dad home?" asked Daviel as he entered the house.

"He is in the den. What's wrong!"

The boys did not hesitate but ran straight to the den. Mrs. McKnight followed them.

"Dad, I have to get to San Pedro immediately!" shouted Daviel.

As he continued to talk the judge said, "Whoa, slow down. Do you mind telling me what this is all about?"

Daviel took a deep breath and then told them about the stolen daggers and the clue that they found. "So, you see dad, I figure they are heading for San Pedro. I have to get there immediately and look for them."

"Hey, what about me!" interjected Hal.

"You too of course; we are a team," said Daviel.

"Have you told the police about this clue?" the judge asked.

"No sir, we came straight here."

The judge called the police and they agreed to send a man right over. He was told that there was not anything new happening with the case and then he hung up the phone.

The boys expectantly looked at the judge. Finally, he said, "I've heard about a missionary family there named the [1] Wyckoff's. They have a church and are starting an orphanage. They live by faith, telling only the Lord their needs and wait for Him to supply."

---

[1]. The Wyckoffs were real missionaries in San Pedro, Mexico

"Great!" shouted Daviel. "Could we call them and see if we could come?"

"It is late and I need to see if I can find a pastor or someone who supports them to get their number. I will do it first thing in the morning, Okay?"

"Sure, dad, I just hope it does not take too long. I want to get my daggers back."

"Go on home and get some sleep. I will try to find out something tonight and we will contact the Wyckoff's in the morning. Besides, Chief Kent said that he would lock down all means of escape."

"That is true dad but there are always the back roads. All the roads out of Savannah cannot be watched."

The boys agreed to the judge's plan and after good-nights and words of 'I love you' were exchanged they went home.

Daviel did not sleep well. All night he made plans about how to get to San Pedro. When he did sleep, he slept fitfully, tossing and turning. He ate very little breakfast. He was so upset that he did not have his devotions nor do his exercises. He and Hal were at the judge's door by nine in the morning.

"I have been trying to find a church that supports the Wyckoff's but have not been successful. I believe that their sending church was in North Carolina, somewhere around the Shelby area. I was just going to get an atlas to see what other cities were near there."

"Dad, we can check on the computer," said Daviel, "It will be faster."

Daviel and Hal brought up the judge's computer. Daviel tried to get him to leave it running but old habits die hard. Something about not wanting to waste electricity.

When it was up and running Daviel keyed in Shelby, North Carolina Map and soon a map displayed of Shelby and its surrounding areas. Next Daviel keyed in Independent Baptist Churches of Shelby and found two. After writing down the information he then keyed in and requested information of any Independent Baptist Churches within fifty miles of Shelby. After writing down the numbers they divided forces and called the churches.

"I got it!" yelled Hal. "Their sending church is Cornerstone Baptist Church, Mooresboro, North Carolina. I do not have them on my list. Do either of you?" asked Hal.

"If you do not have the church on your list then how do you know they are from that church?" asked Judge McKnight.

"I talked with a Pastor Camp and he told me. Now, who has the number?"

"I have it," declared the judge. "Hold on while I call."

While the judge called and while they waited for someone to answer the phone Hal paced the floor. No one answered so the judge left an urgent message.

"Why don't you boys drive around and see if you can pick up any clues," suggested the Judge.

"That is a great idea. You will call us as soon as you hear something right?" questioned Daviel.

Laughing the judge said, "Of course, now get going."

They went to the island's garage on the mainland and decided to take Hals car since it was black. Hal drove.

"Where should we start?" he asked Daviel.

"I would suggest that we go to some of the more, shady areas of town. If those clowns are in hiding then I doubt they would be in the Carlton Hotel."

"That sounds logical," said a grinning Hal.

"What are you grinning at?"

Hal simply smiled and thought, *Daviel is always so practical.*

Hal drove to a not so nice section of town. This area was known for its many knife fights and drug wars.

"I hope you know what you are doing," Hal whispered.

"Why are you whispering? No one can hear us," laughed Daviel.

"Well, you must admit that this area is not the greatest and has a rather infamous reputation."

"That is why we are here. They would not hide in a good area, not with the police looking for them. I just hope they have not already gone to Mexico."

"I doubt it," responded Hal. "They will probably lie low for a few days, you know, until the heat is off."

"You sound more like a detective every day," Daviel declared.

The boys kept their windows up and the doors locked. As the new car drove down the trash filled streets people stared and even pointed at it. Hal was glad for the dark tinted windows.

Daviel and Hal drove through several run–down areas but did not spot the thieves. In one area they were chased by another car. A very scared Hal drove like a maniac trying to lose the car. After driving down several streets he saw his chance. At the last minute he made a hair pin turn down a side street praying it was not a dead end. The car following his was taken by surprise by the daring move and passed the street. By the time their pursuer turned around Hal had managed to escape. Both boys were nervous.

"You know Hal," started Daviel, "if we want to be detectives, we had better take karate lessons — soon!"

Hal nodded his head in agreement.

"We might as well head back to dad's house. If those men are still in Savannah, they will not be showing their faces," Daviel said.

Hal drove back to the judge's house and parked on the street. He and Daviel did not bother to knock but just entered. The judge was talking on the phone.

After he hung up Daviel asked, "Who were you talking to dad?"

"That was Dana, the pastor's wife at Cornerstone. I have the Wyckoff's phone number."

Daviel and Hal were very excited.

"Calm down while I make the call."

Judge McKnight dialed the number and waited while it rang. After ten rings he hung up.

"I guess they don't have an answering machine," he said. "We will try again in an hour. So how did your search go?"

"We are lucky to be alive!" declared Hal.

Judge McKnight raised his eyebrows but said nothing. He was use to Hal's exaggerations.

Hal explained about the car following them. The judge listened and smiled as Hal told him what happened. The judge was pretty sure that Hal embellished some of his story.

"We drove through some pretty seedy parts of town," Daviel admitted, "but did not see anything. Have the police called today?"

"No, not yet, but then they won't unless they know something. Why don't you boys go for a swim in the secret cove? I will call you if I hear anything from the police or if I make contact with the Wyckoff's."

"Yes sir, that will keep us occupied," said a dejected Daviel,

He and Hal went swimming in the secret cove but somehow Daviel was not as enthusiastic about his beautiful cove. After swimming they went to the mansion and watched some videos. They waited all day and all evening but no calls came. At ten Daviel's dad called and told them to go to bed. He would try the Wyckoff's again in the morning.

At nine the next morning the boys entered the McKnight's home again.

"Hey dad, we are here. Have you heard anything?" questioned Daviel.

"Are you packed?" asked the judge.

"Packed?" echoed the boys.

"That's what I asked. We are going to San Pedro. I talked with Mr. Wyckoff and he said for us to come. We have reservations to fly from Savannah to Houston and from Houston straight to Torreon. Our plane leaves at one o'clock so you boys had better get packed. Hal, I talked with your parents last night. They are giving me a letter of permission for you to go too."

"Yippee!" Shouted the two excited boys. "We will go and pack right now," said Daviel.

As the boys ran to the front door, they both suddenly stopped. "Thanks!" they said in unison and continued on their way.

The judge called police headquarters but there was not anything new to report. The thieves had not been caught and there was no sign of them. They did contact the police in San Pedro and the theft was broadcast nationwide.

The ride to the airport, although a short one, was very quiet. At one, they boarded the plane for Houston.

"Do you have my letter of permission?" asked Hal for the hundredth time. (A minor who was going to Mexico with someone other than his parents had to have a notarized letter of permission from his parents in order to enter Mexico.)

They had a good flight to Houston and were waiting to change planes for Torreon. The delay was supposed to be for thirty minutes and after an hour the judge asked what the hold-up was.

"I am sorry sir, but the plane scheduled to go to Torreon has engine problems. We are trying to locate another plane. I apologize for the delay," said the ticket agent.

When the people around the room heard that the plane had engine problems and that they were trying to locate another plane they started murmuring.

After waiting another two hours the judge called the Wyckoff's and informed them of the problem. He told them that he would call as soon as they knew something.

Finally, after a three-hour delay, another plane was located and was pulling up to the terminal.

"May I have your attention please? All passengers to Torreon, Mexico and then on to Mexico City, your plane is ready for boarding. Please have your tickets ready and begin boarding. Thank you!"

"All right! That is us!" shouted Daviel.

"Daviel calm down," said Hal. "I am the impatient one not you!"

Daviel gave him a short laugh and said, "I know Hal but the more time we waste here at the airport the more time the thieves have to get away. Those daggers are important to me."

"I know they are son, but worrying about them will not bring them back any quicker. The airline did everything possible."

"I know dad, I am sorry. Come on, let us get aboard."

As they were presenting their tickets to the ticket checker, they were told that the plane was failing its preflight check and they would have to wait for another plane. She was sorry for the inconvenience.

A very disappointed Daviel went to sit down and wait some more. The judge led the group to some chairs in the corner of the first-class lounge where they would have some privacy.

"Daviel, did the stealing of your daggers and the plane problems take God by surprise?" asked the judge.

"No sir, but—"

"There are no 'buts' with God, Daviel. He is in control or He isn't. We have to trust Him."

"I know dad and you are right but it is hard. I am sorry."

"Remember when you first inherited the money; do you remember what I told you?"

"No sir."

"Daviel, so far in your young life," (Daviel smiled at the word young), "you have been able to handle everything that has come your way. I know that you read your Bible daily and pray and are walking close to the Lord. Remember I told you that you would need to depend on the Lord and not your money and that—"

"Oh dad!" interrupted Daviel. "My first real test comes and I blow it. I am so sorry."

"Don't' tell me your sorry; tell the Lord."

Right there in the airport Daviel bowed his head and prayed, "Lord, please forgive me for my lack of confidence in You. My first real test comes and I fail, please Lord forgive me and help me to always remember this day. You know Lord how important those daggers are to me. I realize You could have kept them from being stolen but You chose not to. Please Lord, help me to rely on You and not me or my money. I put the whole thing in Your hands and if You desire for me to have the daggers back, great, and if not, thank You for the peace which only You can give. Please give us wisdom to do what You want us to do and please Lord guide the police. Amen."

Daviel looked up after his prayer and smiled. He felt the Lord's presence and knew that everything would be okay whether he got the daggers back or not.

Thirty minutes later the ticket agent announced that the passengers on flight 609 bound for Torreon and then Mexico City would need to go to terminal C11 to catch a different flight. Of course, she was sorry for the inconvenience.

Daviel, Hal, and the judge left for the other end of their concourse. Soon all the passengers were boarded and the plane was taxiing for the runway. They only went about one hundred yards when the plane turned around and headed for the terminal again. The passengers sat on the plane for half an hour and then were told to please re-enter the terminal.

Judge McKnight asked what was the problem?

He was told that this plane too was experiencing engine problems and that they would have to wait until tomorrow for another plane.   The airlines would put everyone up for the night in a hotel.

The passengers grabbed their carry-on luggage and followed a stewardess to a waiting shuttle bus to the airport. Daviel's dad could see that his son was disappointed but was handling it well.

After checking into the hotel, he said, "Well son, you took that news very well. I am proud of you."

"Well dad I have to admit that I am disappointed but I did turn it over to the Lord so I know that He has a reason for our delay. What are we going to do until tomorrow?"

"First I need to call the Wyckoff's and tell them of our delay. After that why don't we go to a really nice restaurant and maybe a show before we turn in for the night? I understand that there is a dinner theatre somewhere around here that is supposed to be really good."

The call to the Wyckoff's was made and after getting directions from the hotel desk clerk the three set out for the dinner theater.

The Lord was with them and they managed to get a seat down front. They quickly ordered and just as their food was being served, they had just enough time to pray before the play began.

The play was a comedy and soon the whole room was laughing between mouths full of food. After dinner the threesome returned to the hotel in very good moods.

"How come we don't have anything like that in Savannah?" asked Hal.

"Really dad, I think that something like that would go over really well. That place was packed!" exclaimed Daviel.

"Well son, maybe you should consider opening up one. I think it would be a big success."

"I would not mind opening up a dinner theater. It could be a lot of fun. I will pray about it. Of course, our restaurant would be a Christian restaurant. The show that we saw tonight would be a good one. I will have to do some research when we get home."

They were all tired from the long delays and the good meal they had eaten and everyone quickly fell asleep. After breakfast in the hotel dining room they headed back to the airport.

They were told that the plane for Torreon would be boarding in thirty minutes and were guaranteed there were not any problems with this plane. They were thanked for their patience and kindness.

The judge again phoned the Wyckoff's and told them their arrival time.

They were flying to Torreon, the closest international airport to San Pedro. Mr. and Mrs. Wyckoff would meet them at the airport.

Two hours after taking off from Houston the plane landed in Torreon. After passing through customs they looked for the Wyckoff's. The "International Airport" was very small with only one concourse and only one gate. They were expecting a huge airport like the Atlanta International Airport and so were very surprised. They had no problem finding Mr. and Mrs. Wyckoff. Soon the two groups were headed to San Pedro in the Wyckoff's van. They spent the next forty-five minutes getting acquainted.

CHAPTER 8
THE WYCKOFF FAMILY

"**D**o you have any children?" asked Hal.

"We have three girls and three boys. Our oldest daughter lives in Texas. They are all excited about meeting you and helping you on your mystery. Right now, they are riding around San Pedro looking for the men. I printed off the pictures that you emailed me. If they are in San Pedro, they will eventually find them. Some friends of theirs are helping them. You must meet the Martínez family while you are here. They have four children – two girls and two boys. They are between thirteen and fifteen years old. My children are twelve to twenty-one years old. The girls are the oldest."

Soon they pulled up in front of a house. A flock of kids came running out. There were five white Americans and five brown skinned Americans from Mexico. The United States and Mexico are both part of North and Central America so all the kids were

Americans. Everyone was introduced to each other and soon a conference was taking place in the living room. "We are so glad that you could come," explained Mr. Wyckoff. "My children tell me that they have visited all the hotels in San Pedro and showed the pictures to all the workers and no one has seen the men. We will have dinner and get acquainted. Tomorrow the children will search some more for the men. They may not have arrived in Mexico yet if they are hiding from the police."

"Tell us about yourself and your ministry," said the Judge.

"We are a faith-based ministry. By that I mean that we tell only the Lord our needs and wait for Him to supply them. Whenever someone asks us: 'Do you need' (whatever it may be) they always get the same response. What is that children?"

"We tell only the Lord our needs. If we have full cupboards or empty cupboards, we always say the same thing; we tell only the Lord our needs," all the children said in unison.

"Why do you do that?" asked Daviel. "How am I or anyone else supposed to know what you need?"

"We do it that way because we believe that God still answers prayer. We want to be a testimony to our prayer answering God. You see, Daviel, if you wanted to send us something here to San Pedro, we probably would not receive it. Therefore, sending us money, not here to Mexico, but to our sending church if you want a tax deduction or to my parents if you do not want a tax deduction is the best way to meet our needs. We tell everyone that if God lays us on your heart then we have a need. If He does not lay us on your heart then we are doing fine. We have never asked anyone for support but the Lord has always laid us on someone's heart whenever we had a need."

"I bet that upsets some people," said Hal.

"Sometimes it does but only because they are worried about us. My parents had a hard time dealing with it but now they are doing fine. It is an exciting way to live. My children have seen God do some wonderful things for us."

Addressing his children he said, "Why don't you show Daviel and Hal their room. I will show Judge McKnight his room later. You can discuss your plans for finding the two men."

The children all went upstairs with the luggage. They sat around the room talking and making plans. They told Daviel and Hal not to drink the water from the faucet. They then told them where the bottled water was kept.

"I think," said Brittany, "that we should watch the hotel San Pedro for the next couple of days. They may be in league with the two men and not be telling us the truth. They may already be there. The rest of us could ride around San Pedro looking for the men. We can communicate by walkie-talkie."

"That sounds like a good plan," said Daviel. "Hal speaks and understands Spanish better than I do. We will walk around and see if we can find the men. That would be okay would it not?"

"Oh, sure, you would be safe but don't you want one of us to go with you?" asked Brianna.

"No! I mean, the men will recognize us and I think that it would be better if we were not seen together. That way you may not cause suspicion where we will if they see us."

"That sounds like a plan," said Elí in Spanish.

That night before going to bed they told the adults their plan and put it into action the next day. They spent two days looking for the men without spotting them.

It was the third day of their search and they were getting discouraged.

Andrés called on the walkie-talkie, "Everyone meet me at the plaza, pronto!"

It took about fifteen minutes but everyone gathered at the plaza. They had a ten-minute conference.

"The men are in the restaurant La Hacienda," began Andrés.

"Are you sure it is them?" asked Azalia.

"They looked just like the pictures," he said and turning to Daviel he asked, "What do you want to do?"

As Daviel was trying to think up a plan the two men left the restaurant.

"Elí," said Daniel, "follow those two men and let us know where they go."

After a short time Elí returned.

"Fueron al Hotel La Hacienda," he reported.

"They went to the Hotel La Hacienda, where is that?" asked Hal.

"Sigueme!" said Elí.

"Wait!" exclaimed James. "Before we follow you and get caught let's send Brittany to the hotel to talk to Sister Elena. She is a very good friend of ours," explained James.

"Brittany," said Daviel, "try to find out what room they are in, okay."

She nodded her head yes as she started for the hotel. Ten minutes later she came back.

"I told Sister Elena everything. She said that we could sit in her patio and wait for the men to leave. After they leave, we can search their room for the daggers. She also called the police. They will be here shortly to arrest the men."

As the young people were about to enter the hotel; the two men left. They divided their forces. Daviel and Hal stayed with the girls to wait for the police while the rest followed the men.

The police finally came and searched the room but the daggers were not there. They made plans to stake out the hotel so the young people left to find the others. After searching for a while, they decided to go back to the Wyckoff's house and get ready for church. They would try again the next day.

The other group had a little more success. They followed the men to the Hotel Misión. There the two men went to room ten and talked to a man.

"Elí," said Daniel. "Do you think that you could stand outside their window and hear what they are saying?"

"Claro que si! (Of course!)," he said and left.

They watched Elí as he stood beside the window and listened to the conversation. He returned when he thought the meeting was ending.

"Did you learn anything?" asked Daniel.

"Muchos, pero vamos a su casa. Es tiempo para el culto." (A lot but let's go to your house. It is time for church.) he said.

He told them what he had overheard as they walked quickly home. Daviel met them at the door but since it was time for church he had to wait until after the service to find out anything. He was a little frustrated. The service seemed to last forever but actually it was over in an hour. Finally, everyone left for their homes and they all had a meeting.

This is what Elí told them. "They have the daggers hidden somewhere. The man that they met wants to buy them. He collects things like that. The men that stole the daggers said that they would meet him at the cave in Tacubaya tomorrow."

"Tacubaya!" shouted the Wyckoff children.

"Do you know where that is?" asked Daviel.

"Yes," said Stephen, "and we know where the cave is. We call it Sand Mountain because it is very sandy there."

"We have also found shells from guns there and we think that maybe a revolution is being planned from there," added James.

"Can we go there early in the morning?" asked Hal.

"Oh, sure," said Daniel. "Dad and mom let us go there all the time. Everyone be here tomorrow at seven o'clock. If you are not here on time, we will leave without you. We will ride our bikes."

CHAPTER 9

SAND MOUNTAIN CAVE

The next day only Andrés was able to come as the others had school. They left for Tacubaya at seven o five.

Daviel told Hal that they needed to use their observation skills in case they had to go to Tacubaya by themselves. Hall nodded his agreement. They rode through San Pedro on the paved roads but soon came to dirt roads.

"I-I-s-s th-th-this th-th-e only way t-t-t-o-o-o T-t-tacubaya-a-a?" asked Daviel while his teeth clicked constantly from the jarring they were taking on the very bumpy road.

"N-n-no b-bb-ut-t it is the sh-sh-shortest," said Daniel.

Finally, they were off the rocky dirt road and on a paved one. They entered the sandy road to Sand Mountain at eight o'clock.

"We will need to be very quiet from now on," said Daniel. "We do not know if they are already here or not."

They decided to walk the bikes to the mountain instead of riding them because it would be quieter. The dirt "road" to the mountain was clear of any tracks so they figured no one was there but with all the wind their tracks could have been covered by the loose blowing sand. After a five-minute walk they hid their bikes behind some trees and then proceeded to climb the mountain of sand up to the cave. Daviel thought, *This would be fun if I were not looking for my daggers.*

"Is this the only way to get to the cave?" asked Daviel.

"We don't know. We have never climbed to the cave before. We have always planned to do it but never have," said James.

"Have you ever climbed to the cave Andrés?" asked Stephen.

"This is my first time to come here. How did you ever find this mountain?" he asked Daniel.

"We were on one of our four-hour bike rides when we found Tacubaya. Dad was with us and we decided to see where this dirt road went. We found what we call Sand Mountain and have been here several times but have never climbed to the cave."

It was a long climb up to the cave and the sand made it difficult at times. There were not any rocks to grab onto and sometimes they would lose their footing and go sliding down the mountain until they could stop. They were having so much fun that they forgot to be quiet. Finally, they reached the cave entrance.

After emptying the sand out of his tennis shoes Daniel asked Brittany, "Did you bring the flash lights?

"Of course, let's go."

They quickly searched the cave as it was not very deep but they found nothing.

Disappointedly Hal asked, "Are there any other caves?"

"Not that we know of," said James.

"Are there any other Sand Mountains?" asked Daviel

Again, the response was *"not that we know of."* They climbed back down the mountain which was quicker than climbing up and hid. Hopefully the two men would come soon. They were in for a big surprise. As they were waiting a group of men came in uniforms and started shooting at the mountain. They were practicing. The soldiers spent the next three hours shooting at targets and climbing the mountains. No one dared to breathe. They were afraid of what might happen to them if they were caught. Finally, the men left.

"I sure am glad that is over," said Brianna. "I am starved!"

They pulled out their lunches and ate them. They waited in hiding for a couple more hours. It was getting late so they decided to head back to the house. Daviel was disappointed but he determined to return the next day.

"Well, what did you boys find out?" asked Judge McKnight when they got home.

They told him and the others about their day.

"Are you sure that there are not any other Sand Mountains around here?" asked Daviel again.

Mr. Wyckoff thought a few minutes before answering. "There are the sand dunes over by Viesca but they are not mountains."

"The only sand mountain or cave in Tacubaya that we know of is the one we went to today," said Stephen.

"How about if we call Sister Elena and see if the two men have returned. Maybe the police picked them up and that is why we did not see them," suggested Brittany.

They made the phone call and were disappointed to learn that the two men had not returned to the hotel but that the police were looking for them.

"Could we maybe go to Viesca and scout around?" asked Hal.

"I guess it would not hurt to go there," said Mr. Wyckoff. "I cannot take you because I have an appointment but you can take the bus."

"Is that safe?" asked the judge.

"Oh sure, besides, my children will be with them. Can you go Andrés?" Mr. Wyckoff asked.

"Yes sir, I have nothing to do right now," replied the boy.

The next day the eight of them boarded a bus for Viesca.

"Boy this bus is ancient!" declared Hal. "How far is Viesca and are you sure this tub will make it?" asked Hal in Spanish and English.

"Tub!" asked Andrés not being familiar with the word.

Brittany explained it to him.

Smiling he said that the 'tub' would make it, but slowly. He then explained that Viesca took about twenty minutes by car but would take an hour by bus. Part of the reason for that was because the bus had many stops on the way there. They enjoyed the hot ride there (no air–conditioning) especially going downhill. The bus managed to go forty–five miles-per-hour downhill but only thirty miles-per-hour uphill. Daviel was thankful that there were not any mountains.

The ride took only fifty-five minutes and was very hot. The temperature inside the bus was over one hundred degrees.

They exited the bus and had to take a taxi to the sand dunes. They were exactly what you would think – sand dunes. There were miles of lovely white sand but no place for a cave. They searched the whole area and returned to Viesca where Daviel bought everyone lunch of gorditas.

"I guess that was a wasted trip," declared James.

"Not really," started Daviel.

"Oh, no, not again. Don't you ever give up?"

"What?" questioned Daviel smiling at his friend.

"You are going to say, 'not really, we spent time together having fun' weren't you.

"I guess big brother that you know me too well. But it is true. It is never a waste of time if it is spent with friends. Too bad we did not bring swim suits. We could have gone swimming in that pool over there.

Everyone looked to where Daviel was pointing.

"I did not know they had a pool here, did you An-drés?"

"No, but then I never come here," he explained.

"If you guys ever get to Savannah, Georgia you have to visit me at my Island. I have the perfect swimming place. It is totally private. Hal and I swim there often. Next time you get to the states let me know and I will send you the money to come."

"You will love Daviel's island," said Hal.

"I guess we should head back," said Brittany. "There are no caves here."

The ride back to San Pedro was a quiet one. As they got off the bus Daviel exclaimed, "What dummies we are! Did not Eli say that the men specifically mentioned Tacubaya. How could I have forgotten that?"

"Si amigo," said Andres.

The others added that we all forget sometimes.

When they returned to the house Mr. Wyckoff reminded his children of their obligation to help Sister Elena tomorrow so they would not be able to return to the mountain. That night before going to sleep, Daviel and Hal made plans to return to Tacubaya and look for more caves. In the morning they told Daviel's dad their plan and then set off on bikes for the mountain. It was not hard to find Tacubaya but the road leading to the mountain was a little bit more difficult to find as they were not paying close attention yesterday and there was more than one road that they could take. After taking a couple of wrong roads they finally found the right one. They walked their bikes down the long road. They hid behind some bushes and scouted the area. It seemed to be deserted. Again, they hid their bikes and climbed up the mountain to the cave.

Cautiously they entered the cave. They had forgotten to bring batteries for the flashlights. Soon they were standing in the dark. "What great detectives we are," scoffed Daviel, "forgetting to bring flash light batteries."

The boys were discussing what to do when a secret door at the back of the cave opened and in walked the two men. Before they could run, the boys were captured and tied up.

"Well, what have we got here," sneered the man with the scar on his face.

He shined the flashlight into the eyes of Daviel. "Why, you're the little rich brat whose daggers we stole," he said laughingly. "What are you doing here?"

The boys remained silent. The other man with the mole under his eye raised his hand to slap them but the other man stopped him.

"Now don't go roughing them up, not yet anyway." Turning to Daviel he said, "Would you like to see the daggers? We have a man coming to buy them in a couple of hours."

He pulled out the beautiful daggers and Daviel said, "Those are my daggers and I want them back."

The two men laughed.

"How did you find out about them anyway?" asked Hal.

"That was easy kid. I was using the phone at a store in Devil's Cove when I overheard an elderly lady mention your daggers. I listened enough to learn where they were and then we made our plans to steal them."

"Hey!" exclaimed the man with the mole. "I recognize you. You were at the restaurant the other day. You," he said pointing to Hal, "stopped by our table to listen to our conversation. I told you Miguel that they were listening to us."

"Guess you were right and I was wrong. Oh well, all's well that ends well. We have the daggers and in a few hours we will be one hundred thousand dollars richer."

After checking the boy's hands and feet to be sure that they were securely tied they carried them through the secret passage.

Miguel lit a lamp and after the boy's eyes adjusted to the light they looked around. They were in a large storage room full of ammunition.

Seeing the astonished look on the boys faces Miguel explained. "This is our personal warehouse. Many people know about this cave but only the two of us know about this secret room."

"What do you plan to do to us?" asked Daviel.

"I have not decided yet but you will be the first to know when I do," said Miguel.

The boys tried to untie themselves but the knots were too tight.

***

When the Wyckoff children returned to the house they asked where Daviel and Hal were. The judge told them that they went to Sand Mountain but that he expected them home any minute. After thirty minutes and no boys they decide to call the police. The police did not take the call seriously and told them to call again in the morning if the boys had not returned.

"Let's take the van to Tacubaya and see if we can find them. Maybe they got a flat tire and are walking home," suggested Mr. Wyckoff.

"But dad, there is more than one way to get to Tacubaya," Stephen said.

"Yes son, that is true, but Hal and Daviel will only know the way that you went yesterday. If they have a flat tire, we will be able to find them. I can drive the way you took them, right?"

"Yes, dad, we took them the quickest way yesterday and it is drivable," explained Brianna.

With all the thorn bushes in the area it was very easy to get a flat tire. Almost every day the Wyckoff children had to patch a tire on one of their bikes.

It took twenty-five minutes to reach the road to Sand Mountain. It was somewhat precarious but Mr. Wyckoff managed to drive down the sandy road to the mountain.

As they jumped out of the van Daniel said, "Let's see if the bikes are in the same hiding place."

The teens all ran to see. Sure enough, the bikes were there. Now they had proof that Daviel and Hal were there somewhere. They tried calling the boys but there was no answer. Finally, they decided to climb the mountain to the cave. Judge McKnight said that he would wait for them by the van. Mr. Wyckoff wanted to go with the young people but he decided to stay with the judge. As the young people climbed the mountain Mr. Wyckoff and the Judge had a prayer meeting.

The teens searched the cave thoroughly and even called the boys names. Daviel and Hal could hear them and made noises but the teens could not hear them. After deciding that the two boys were not there the Wyckoff children left and climbed to the top of the mountain to scout around. They could not see anyone.

"I wonder where they are," said Brittany.

"They have to be here because their bikes are here," said James.

"Not if they were kidnapped," suggested Brianna.

The others looked at her. "Well it could have happened!" she said.

They went back down the mountain and reported that they could not find the missing boys. They then drove straight to police headquarters.

Chapter 10
ESCAPE

The kidnappers did not see the van leave as they entered the cave from the back entrance. While the others were going for the police the two men were talking to the boys.

"What are we going to do with them?" Raul asked Miguel.

"I have not decided yet. We could leave them here until they die. We could bury them out in the desert or – I guess there really isn't an or – because if we let them live, they will tell where our secret hideout is."

"We promise, we won't tell!" exclaimed Hal.

"Sure kid, you may not tell, but somehow I think the little rich boy would. Ain't that right rich boy," taunted Miguel.

Daviel stared at the man but said nothing. While they were sitting there alone after hearing their friend's voices, he had been desperately trying to free his hands. He thought that the ropes were a little looser but he could not be sure. He just glared at his captors.

Miguel grabbed Daviel's dark red hair and slung his head back so that he could better see the boy's face. Raul was going to slap the boy but Miguel stopped him.

"I was thinking Raul that we could hold this little rich boy for ransom. That would probably bring us a few million dollars. How about it, kid, would your parents pay a few million dollars for you?"

"My parents are dead," proclaimed Daviel. "Only I can get the money out of my account and I will never pay you a penny," he spouted.

The captors thought about that for a minute. "I think I know a way to get that money from you," said Miguel.

He pulled a knife from his pocket and walked over to Hal. "I bet if I cut this pretty boy up a bit you would change your mind."

Hal's eyes were as big as saucers as the knife came closer and closer to his face. Hal did not realize how good looking he was but he surely did not want a bunch of scars on his face.

"Touch him with that knife and I surely will not pay you one penny. I will make a deal with you. I will buy my daggers for one hundred and fifty thousand dollars. That is a fifty-thousand-dollar profit. What do you say?"

"Kid, nice try, but I think that the old man you call dad would pay, at the least, one million dollars for you. Just think Raul, with all that money we could retire and live like kings."

"Yeah Miguel, I like it!"

The two thieves, now turned kidnappers, taunted the boys for a while but when neither boy responded they decided to go outside and look for their buyer. Fortunately, they did not take the daggers with them.

Daviel whispered to Hal. "I think that the rope around my hands is looser. I will try to slide out my hand. If I get loose, I will untie my feet, get the daggers and cut you lose. We will have to run out the back way."

"But we do not know where that leads," said Hal.

"It will lead us away from them and that is what matters."

"Okay," Hal agreed.

Daviel worked for ten minutes trying to get his hands free. His wrists and hands were being rubbed raw but he refused to give up. Finally, his hand slipped out. Quickly he untied his legs, grabbed the daggers and cut Hal free. They were running down the tunnel when they heard a yell.

"After them!" shouted Miguel. "We must catch them quickly. Mr. Escobar is coming up the mountain."

The boys stumbled along as fast as they could down the dark tunnel. The two men who knew the tunnel well were quickly gaining on them.

"Hurry!" exclaimed Hal. "They are gaining on us."

"Look!" shouted Daviel, "I can see a light down there. Let us run faster and pray that we can out run them once we are outside."

"Come back you brats!" yelled Miguel. "I swear I will kill you for this."

The boys put on an extra burst of speed. They reached the exit, pushed open the door and ran for their lives.

"Hal, follow me. We have to get to our bikes!"

Daviel ran towards the cave opening not knowing that Mr. Escobar was coming up the mountain. When he and Hal reached the mountain side with the cave opening, they jumped into the soft sand and started sliding down at a quick pace.

"Mr. Escobar, stop those boys, they have the daggers!" yelled Miguel.

Mr. Escobar grabbed for the boys but they were moving too fast. The end came somewhat quickly as the boys hit the harder packed ground. Both boys rolled and quickly got to their feet and ran for their bikes. They heard Mr. Escobar sliding down the mountain after them.

"Hurry Hal, we have to get away," called Daviel over his shoulder.

Both boys pedaled as fast as they could until they were far enough away and Mr. Escobar could not catch them.

It was hard pedaling through the sandy road but the boys managed to reach the paved main road. Hal looked behind them but did not see any pursuers. Quickly the boys headed for San Pedro. They had no idea what had become of Miguel and Raul.

***

"You morons!" shouted Mr. Escobar. "Now what are you going to do? There is no telling where those boys are going."

"Don't worry Mr. Escobar, we will get the daggers back," consoled Raul.

"You fools! We have no idea where those boys are. Who are they anyway?"

"The red headed one is Daviel. We stole the daggers from him in the states. The black-haired boy is his best friend. I am sure they are heading for San Pedro," Raul said.

"Even if they get back to the states with the daggers, we will steal them again," said Miguel.

He really was not interested in the daggers any more. He had bigger fish to fry. Five million dollars compared to a measly one hundred thousand sounded much better to him. He was sure the boy's father would pay five million to get him back.

"I am returning to my home," said Mr. Escobar. "If you ever steal those daggers again you know where to contact me. Goodbye!"

Taking the roundabout way to avoid capture; Daviel and Hal rode up to the Wyckoff's house two hours later. They entered the gate and hurried into the house. Everyone was surprised to see them.

"Daviel, Hal!" yelled the judge, "I am so glad that you are safe! Is that the daggers?" he asked.

"Yes, sir, could we have something to drink. We are dying of thirst."

After drinking some cold water, the boys looked out the window.

"What are you looking at?" asked Stephen.

"I am checking to see if Miguel or Raul followed us. They are the two thieves."

Satisfied that the coast was clear the boys started shaking from the excitement.

"You boys had better sit down," said Mrs. Wyckoff. "Daviel, what happened to your wrists?"

Daviel, for the first time, noticed the raw marks on his wrists. "They had us tied up. I managed to escape."

Sitting on the sofa the boys managed to relax and tell everyone what had happened while Mrs. Wyckoff put some soothing cream on Daviel's wrists.

"Could we see the daggers?" asked Daniel. He was interested in knives.

Daviel handed the package that he still had clutched in his hands to Daniel who carefully opened it.

"WOW!" he exclaimed.

Everyone got to hold the daggers and everyone remarked about how beautiful they were.

"They must be worth a fortune!" exclaimed Brianna. "How much are they worth?"

"Brianna!" scolded her sister Brittany, "You don't ask questions like that!"

"That is okay, I do not mind. They are worth one million dollars and those imbeciles were going to sell them for only one hundred thousand dollars," said Daviel.

He and Hal were calming down. "Now what are we going to do dad?" asked Daviel.

"I do not know son. Do you have any suggestions?" he asked Mr. Wyckoff.

"Those men have no idea where you are. You can stay here with us until it is time to catch your plane."

"We can't do that," said Hal. When everyone looked at him, he explained, "Miguel decided that after he sold the daggers, he was going to hold Daviel ransom for one million dollars."

"WOW! Are you millionaires?" asked Stephen.

Before Brittany could chastise her brother's ill manners Daviel said, "Yes, I am," and he then explained how he got all of his money.

"I bet you boys are hungry. It is getting late but I could fix you a light snack before you go to bed. You will sleep better with something in your stomach," said Mrs. Wyckoff.

After a light snack everyone went to bed. Daviel slept with his daggers but not before thanking the Lord for giving them back to him.

Chapter 11

GOING HOME

Miguel was furious at the loss of the daggers but more so at the loss of the rich kid. He decided that he would definitely ask for five million dollars after he kidnapped the rich brat again.

"Now what are we going to do?" asked Raul. "Mr. Escobar sure is mad at us."

"The way I figure it is that the daggers are chump change. We need to kidnap the boy and make daddy pay a big ransom for him. However, before we do anything, we need to move our supplies tonight before that kid comes back with the police."

The two men loaded a large truck with all their weapons. They drove through the night to another city and deposited the arms in an abandoned warehouse.

"It sure is good that you had this backup plan," said Raul.

Raul was not very bright but he was loyal. That was the only reason Miguel kept him.

"The way I figure it Raul, the boys must be in San Pedro. How else would they know about Tacubaya. We only mentioned it at the Hotel Misión. I think we should go back there and snoop around. Maybe we will get lucky. We will have to be careful though because the police probably have our description by now."

***

In the morning Daviel asked his dad, "What should I do with the daggers? Do you think they will try and steal them again?"

"Who knows son. They have no way of knowing that we are in San Pedro. Of course, that would be the logical assumption but they would be crazy to come back here."

"Your daggers will be safe here," said Mr. Wyckoff. "No one will get past our dogs."

Daviel smiled at that. Their biggest dog named Precious still would not let him pet her. We only have three more days, thought Daviel. Surely, we will be gone before they can figure out where we are or how to get the daggers again.

Daviel, Hal, Judge McKnight and Mr. Wyckoff went to the police station to report their escape and give them as much information as they could about

Miguel and Raul. They also informed them of Mr. Escobar.

The next two days passed quickly. Only one more day before they went home. Preparations were made for a celebration, a fiesta. The police officers were invited.

"Mexicans love fiestas. Everyone comes to them. Tomorrow we will have chatara, a favorite of my children," said Mrs. Wyckoff.

"Your children eat scrap metal?" asked Hal. "That is what chatara means – scrap metal."

"No," laughed the Wyckoff family, "it is also called discada. It is made on an old disc harrow that was used for tilling up the ground. It is made into a cooking utensil. You build a fire under it and cook the food in it," explained Mr. Wyckoff.

"What all goes in chatara?" asked Daviel. "Neither Hal nor I are picky eaters but we like to know what we are eating. It is not anything like pig brain is it?"

Laughing the girls told him what was in it. "It is made of potatoes, tomatoes, carrots, beef, pork, onion, ham, hot dogs and we add broccoli, cauliflower, and pineapple, V8 juice, and chipotle sauce. Oh yeah it also has jalapeño peppers. Some people put beer in theirs. We don't. You can add any ingredients that you want to but the first ones are the normal ones. We like ours with more vegetables."

"It sounds great to me!" declared Daviel.

"Yeah, me too," seconded Hal. "When do we eat?"

Daviel and Hal helped cut up the meat and vegetables. While they were doing that, others set up tables and decorations.

They had a large fiesta, paid for by Daviel and celebrated long into the night. They had to borrow another disc so that they could make one really spicy hot and the other one normal. By six o'clock the chatara or discada was done.

The Wyckoff children told them that you did not use forks or spoons when eating discada. They showed the boys and the judge how to use their tortillas. For dessert, they had several types of cakes including tres leches which is a cake with three different types of milk in the ingredients. It was very moist and very good. During the fiesta everyone exchanged stories and finally the officers had the story from start to finish.

"I must commend you both on your detective work. Have you thought about being detectives?" asked the officer.

"Hal and I have talked about opening our own detective agency. We are talking about going to a detective school by our house but we mostly are praying to see what the Lord wants us to do."

Daviel spent the next fifteen minutes witnessing to the police officers. They listened politely but did not accept the Lord as their Savior. At least the seed was planted and Mr. Wyckoff could water it later. Who knows, maybe someday it would bear fruit.

Tomorrow, Saturday, was their day to fly home. The government of Mexico gave Daviel a special letter of explanation so that he would not have any trouble bringing the daggers into the United States. He also had letters from the police in Savannah Georgia.

They enjoyed their visit with the Wyckoff family and Daviel wanted to reward them for their help but Mr. Wyckoff would not let him.

"We were glad to be of some help to you. We hope that you will come back and visit us again."

Daviel and Hal promised to do that. As they were getting on the plane Daviel shook Mr. Wyckoff's hand leaving a large amount of pesos in it. "I will be praying about how I may help you in your ministry. I promise that I will do whatever the Lord tells me to do."

"That is all that any of us can do," replied Mr. Wyckoff.

The whole Wyckoff family saw them off. They exchanged email addresses and promised to keep in touch.

Soon the plane was landing at the Houston airport.   The head of police security met them as they unloaded from the plane.

"If you would not mind sir, please come with me."

They followed the man into a private room.

"What is this all about?" inquired the judge.

"Oh, there is no problem," explained the man. "We need to examine your suitcases and I thought that you may not want everyone to know about the daggers and this room is private."

"Thank you for your courtesy," said the Judge.

The custom's officials admired the daggers and congratulated Daviel on retrieving them. He did not even have to show the letters to the officials. They said that they knew all the details and they were sorry the two men had not been caught.

They boarded another flight and headed for Savannah. Thank the Lord they had no engine problems and were soon landing in Savannah, Georgia. Having already gone through customs in Houston they were free to head home.

There was a big party when they got to the mansion. All of their friends were there including Rita and Pam.

The next day at church Hal and Daviel were heroes. They gloried in the attention but were ready to settle down for school in a couple of weeks.

CHAPTER 12
KIDNAPPED

Two days later Daviel received an email from the Wyckoff's. It said that the buyer for the daggers had been caught.

Daviel was glad. He and Hal sat in the theater room staring at the daggers on the wall.

"Are you going to leave them there?" asked Hal.

"Yes I am. That is where they belong. I think that I will get a couple of guard dogs though. What kind do you think I should get?"

The boys talked about different breeds of dogs and drifted off to sleep. Daviel's favorite breed was the Saint Bernard but they were not the best guard dogs though they were big. Miguel and Raul still had not been captured but Daviel felt that his daggers would be safe. Someone was always at the mansion and with the newly installed security system he felt secure.

It has often been said that when we let down our guard something bad happens. One evening Daviel left his island to go to Hal's house. No one knew where Miguel and Raul were and Daviel felt that they could not possibly be in Savannah. The police were still looking for them.

Daviel moored the boat at the dock and headed down to Hal's house. Hal was expecting him.

When Daviel was ten minutes late Hal called the mansion and found out that Daviel left twenty minutes ago and should have arrived earlier than expected which was normal for Daviel.

Hal called the Judge and he, the judge, and his father walked to the boat dock. Daviel's boat was moored at the dock. They slowly walked back to the house looking for clues. Mr. Scott found Daviel's cell phone in the grass beside the road.

Judge McKnight called the police. Police Chief Kent sent two of his detectives to look for clues. They did not find any.

Judge McKnight went home and told his wife about Daviel's disappearance and then called Daviel's aunts and uncles. He called the pastor who called the members of the church and got the prayer chain started. Someone would be praying for Daviel twenty-four hours a day.

Chief Kent came to the judge's house and spent the night. He wanted to be there if a ransom-call came in.

Early the next morning Hal entered the judge's house and asked if they had heard anything. He looked really haggard. It was obvious that he did not get very much sleep.

Hal paced back and forth across the living room floor. Mrs. McKnight said, "Do sit down dear before you wear a hole in the carpet."

"Yes ma'am" he said as he sat down for ten seconds and started pacing again. "Why aren't the police doing something," he asked Chief Kent.

"What would you like us to do Hal? Until the McKnights receive a ransom call there is nothing we can do. There are not any clues."

"What about Miguel and Raul!" accused Hal. "They have to be the kidnappers. Why haven't you found them yet?"

Judge McKnight put his arm around the boy's shoulders. "I know how close you and Daviel are and I know that this is hard for you. It is hard for Mrs. McKnight and me, but we have to trust the Lord. He has allowed this for a reason."

"I know, I know, but I feel so useless. I should be doing something." Turning to Chief Kent he said, "I'm sorry sir. I know that you and your men are doing all that you can. I just —" Hal could not say anymore; he was too choked up.

Judge McKnight held the boy until he was all cried out. Tears were running down the judge's face. "All we can do is pray and trust God to do what is best. We do not know for sure that Miguel and Raul have Daviel. The police have been looking for them and feel sure that they are not in Savannah."

"I know that and that is what scares me. If they don't have him, then who does?"

No one could answer that question.

✳✳✳

In an abandoned shack in Richmond Hill, Daviel was trying to get free from the ropes around his wrists. His kidnappers tied him really tight not wanting him to escape. He was lying on his stomach with his hands tied behind his back. The rope went from his wrists, around his neck, and was tied to his ankles. His legs were bent at the knees. If he moved too much the rope around his neck tightened and cut off his circulation.

"You might as well give it up before you strangle yourself," sneered one of his kidnappers.

"Never." said a determined Daviel. He would rather die trying to escape than give in.

"Suit yourself," said the other kidnapper who was busy cutting words out of a newspaper to make a ransom note. "Soon your papá will be paying big bucks to get his baby boy back."

"My dad and I have a deal. He will not pay you anything to get me back. We do not crash under pressure."

"Well for your sake kid I hope you are wrong. We may have lost the daggers but we now have a much bigger fish. Your papá will pay the five–million–dollar ransom if he wants to see you again – alive."

Daviel jerked at the knots again. For the hundredth time he wished he had already taken karate lessons. He might have been able to defend himself. The best he could do was throw his cell phone into the grass. Hopefully Hal would find it and get the police started searching for him immediately.

Who are you kidding? Daviel asked himself. After being knocked out he had no idea where he was. He could be in Mexico for all he knew though he doubted it.

After struggling for a few more minutes he calmed down. I must remain calm he thought and look for an opportunity to escape, he told himself.

Raul yanked his head back, stared into Daviel's face, and laughed. He then dropped Daviel's head which hit the hard wood floor with a thud. Daviel refused to cry out although his head was hurting.

"Hey, don't damage the merchandise. That boy is valuable," said Miguel.

"Aw don't worry boss. I won't do too much damage. Besides, the punk needs to learn some lessons about who is in control here," said Raul.

"He has spirit, I must say that," said Miguel.

***

The morning passed slowly and still no word from the kidnappers. Hal spent an agonizing two days, and was about at the end of his wits when the ransom note finally came.

It was made up of words from a newspaper that were pasted to the paper. The postmark on the envelope was blurred and of no help. The ransom note said:

IF YOU WANT TO SEE YOUR BOY AGAIN, ALIVE, PLACE FIVE MILLION DOLLARS IN ONE HUNDRED DOLLAR BILLS IN A SUIT CASE AND WAIT FOR FURTHER INSTRUCTIONS.

"Will you pay the ransom demand?" asked Chief Kent.

Judge McKnight looked at Hal before answering, "Daviel and I have an agreement. We have agreed to never pay a ransom demand. We—"

"What!" yelled Hal. "You have to pay the ransom or they will kill Daviel! You have to pay it. Why didn't I accept the money when Daviel offered it to me?" whined Hal. "Then I would have been able to pay the ransom!"

Hal's dad took him into his arms and tried to quiet the emotional boy. The Judge's heart went out to the boy.

"Hal, I know that you know Daviel's wishes about paying a ransom demand. I have heard the two of you talking about it. I have never promised Daviel that I would not pay the money. I only agreed to consider it. Daviel is afraid that if we pay one kidnapper a ransom that others will try. I have to pray and see what God wants me to do."

Hal stared at the judge. Everything the judge said was true. He and Daviel had talked about it and Daviel knew that if he could Hal would pay the ransom no questions asked.

"What are we going to do dear?" asked Mrs. McKnight. "Daviel is worth way more than five million dollars."

"Yes dear, I know that. I would pay everything I have to get him back. He is priceless, but it is Daviel's money and we have to take his feelings into consideration."

During the next two days Rita called continuously. She tried to keep a positive attitude although her heart was breaking. "Please Lord, let Daviel be okay. You know how much he means to me and I know that he means even more to You. Help me to place him in Your hands. Thank You Lord."

***

Daviel's muscles ached. He had quit trying to get free a long time ago. Now he was simply trying to survive the agony in his muscles. He had been tied in his current position for two days. He survived by thinking about his parents, Rita, and Hal. He knew that Hal would be going crazy.

"Listen kid, if you promise not to try anything stupid, I will cut your bonds and tie you in a more comfortable position," said Miguel.

"Thank you," was all he said.

When Miguel cut the ropes and freed Daviel's arms and legs his muscles screamed in revolt. He tried not to cry out but the pain was too great. He managed to only moan and rub his shoulders and other sore muscles.

Miguel carried the boy over to the bed and took off his shirt. "I admire your grit kid. This cream should help with the sore muscles." Miguel rubbed the cream into Daviel's muscles and it did help. He also gave the boy some aspirins for the pain.

After putting his shirt back on Daviel asked, "Why are you being so nice to me all of a sudden?"

"As I said, I admire your grit. I also need you in good shape tomorrow when we call your dad. I hope for your sake he has the money."

"I already told you that we have an agreement. He will not pay a ransom for me."

"Why not kid? That does not make sense," said Miguel.

"I told my dad to never pay a ransom for me because if someone saw that a ransom was paid then they might get the idea into their head to kidnap me for a ransom. It would never end! By not paying the ransom no one else will kidnap me"

Raul who had been listening to this conversation walked over to Daviel and said, "You got that right kid. No one else will kidnap you because you will be dead! I sure hope you are wrong boy. It would give me great pleasure to rough you up a bit but I don't want Miguel to get mad at me. However, if your daddy don't pay, I will enjoy hurting you."

"As you can see, Raul has a nasty streak and he loves to hurt people. When you talk to your dad tomorrow you better convince him to pay," encouraged Miguel.

Daviel's mind was working fast. He had to find a way out. He knew that tomorrow his muscles would be sorer than they were now. What could he do? Maybe he could get the two men mad at each other. If they got to fighting maybe he could escape, he thought.

Daviel decided that he had better pretend to behave so that he would not be tied up like he was before. At bedtime Raul wanted to retie him as before but Miguel said that they only needed to tie his arms behind his back. He said that Daviel's muscles would be too sore to try anything. Daviel was ecstatic but he did not show it.

✳✳✳

Many of the church members either called or came by to tell them that they were praying. Somehow the press had heard about the kidnapping and were clamoring for attention. Pastor Jones and his wife came to the house to offer comfort and prayer.

Rita called often. Because of all the press her parents felt she should not try and go to the McKnight's house. She was worried about not hearing from the kidnappers. What were they doing to Daviel? Because of this crisis she realized that Daviel meant more to her than she had thought.

Hal was beside himself with worry. Being impetuous he wanted to be doing something, but what? He had no idea where Daviel was. The six o'clock news did not help. They announced Daviel's kidnapping but had no other information. They speculated that Daviel was dead or there would have been word from the kidnappers by now. This only made Hal more upset so he turned off the TV.

At nine thirty the call came.

"Let me speak to the judge," said a voice with an obvious Mexican accent.

"This is the judge."

"Do you have the money?" asked the voice.

"Before I say yes or no, I want to talk to Daviel. How do I know that he is even alive?"

"You will have to take my word for it. Do you have the money?" After a pause the voice said, "Listen mister, if you want to see your boy again, alive that is, then don't make me mad. For the last time, do you have the money?"

"I already told you, I want to talk to Daviel. If you hurt one hair on my son's head there will be no place for you to hide," said the judge calmly. "I will hunt you down like the scum you are."

To the judge's surprise the kidnapper laughed. "I now know where that boy of yours gets his grit. So, you want to talk to him. Here!"

"Daviel, are you there?"

"Hi dad, it is I. I am fine."

"Have they hurt you?" asked the judge.

"Stop stalling," yelled a voice.

"Dad, do not pay the ransom, I'd rather they—"

The judge heard a slap and then the phone fell to the floor. "Listen old man, you had better pay the ransom or I promise you, you will never see your son again alive," said an angry voice. "Now do you have the ransom money."

"If you hurt my boy —"

"Shut up old man. You have until noon tomorrow to get that money. I will call at noon with directions and if you don't have the money the boy dies!"

The phone call was abruptly cut off.

"Were you able to trace the call?" asked a detective.

"Sort of sir, the call came from Richmond Hill but we do not know where in Richmond Hill," said a police woman.

"Get me the police chief in Richmond Hill!" shouted Chief Kent.

"Yes sir!"

The woman called the long–distance operator and placed a call to Richmond Hill. "Police Chief Benson's office, officer Kiley speaking."

"Officer Kiley this is police Chief Kent of Savannah. We just received a ransom call for Daviel Amberstcrombie and it came from somewhere in Richmond Hill. Have you guys seen anything suspicious out there?"

"No sir, we have been searching for the boy and the kidnappers but have not found anything. I will call Chief Benson and have him call you."

"Thank you, Officer Kiley. Goodbye!"

"Mr. McKnight you have to pay the ransom. They will kill Daviel if you don't!" shouted Hal. "How can you think about not paying? Don't you love Daviel?" he accused.

"Hal!" shouted Mr. Scott. "You apologize right now to the judge."

Hal looked like he would rebel but he said, "I'm sorry sir, I know that you love Daviel, it's just that I am so worried. Please pay the ransom."

"Don't worry Hal, I will pay the ransom, in fact the bank already has it ready but I had to try Daviel's way first. I agree, they will kill him if they don't get the money."

Hal sank into a chair relieved that the judge was going to pay the ransom demand. While everyone in the room talked, a plan formulated in his mind. Quietly he slipped from the room. No one saw him leave.

CHAPTER 13
HAL TO THE RESCUE

The phone rang again. "Hello,"

"This is Police Chief Benson, is Chief Kent there?"

"One moment sir," said the judge.

"Chief Kent speaking; what have you got for me?"

"We are searching Richmond Hill again. It will take about an hour. Are you sure the call came from here?" asked Chief Benson.

"We had the kidnapper on the phone long enough to determine the call came from there but not long enough to find out where. We will wait for you to call us back."

After the chief hung up Mrs. McKnight entered with some hot coffee. "Coffee anyone?" she asked.

"Thanks darling," replied her husband. They looked into each other's eyes and smiled. As hard as it was, they knew that they had to trust the Lord to do what was best for them and Daviel.

Everyone waited for the hour to pass. Quietly they shared their ideas and plans to get Daviel back. After discussing their options for an hour and before Chief Benson called Mr. Scott turned around and started to ask Hal a question. "Where's Hal!" he exclaimed.

Everyone turned and looked at the chair Hal had been sitting in.

"Did anyone hear him leave?" asked the judge.

"This is great, just great!" moaned Chief Kent. "Now we have two boys missing."

"Calm down chief," encouraged the judge. "He may be upstairs or he may have gone to his house or the island."

"I'll check upstairs," volunteered Mrs. McKnight.

"I'll check our house," said Mrs. Scott.

"I will call the mansion and see if he is there," offered the judge.

Hal was not upstairs, nor at his house, nor was he at the mansion. No one had seen him.

Looking at Mr. Scott the judge asked, "Are you thinking what I am thinking?"

"I am sure that I am. He went after the kidnappers. He's on his way to Richmond Hill!"

"But honey," said Mrs. Scott, "Hal has no money."

"Money won't be a problem. Hal knows that Daviel keeps five hundred thousand dollars in his room safe in case of an emergency. He also knows the combination," said the judge before calling Uncle Jim.

"Jim, this is Judge McKnight. I need you to go to Daviel's room and open the safe. I suspect Hal took the money and has gone to Richmond Hill. Yes, I'll hold."

Everyone in the room was quiet while the judge waited for Uncle Jim to return. It only took a couple of minutes but seemed like forever.

"Judge, the money is gone!"

"Oh no," groaned the judge. "Thanks Jim." Hanging up the phone he said, "The money is gone."

"How would he get to Richmond Hill?" asked Chief Kent.

"He could have taken his car, or Daviel's car or one of our cars," said Hal's father. "He may have taken a bus knowing that you would put out an APB on whichever car he took."

"We need to know how he went. Please check all possibilities and let me know which he chose."

The phone rang. It was Chief Benson. "I am sorry Chief Kent but we came up empty again. There is no sign of Daviel or the kidnappers."

"Thanks Chief, but we may have another prob-lem. Hal, Daviel's best friend is missing. We think he may be headed for or is in Richmond Hill."

"Oh great! What does Hal look like?" asked Chief Benson.

"He is sixteen but looks fourteen, straight black hair, bright large blue eyes with very long eye lashes, five feet six inches tall, weighs one hundred thirty pounds, and looks like he should be a movie star. Unless he changed clothes, he is wearing blue jeans, a red t–shirt, and tennis shoes."

"No, I do not think he is armed. Hold on a minute. His dad just told me that his thirty–eight pistol is missing so consider him to be armed. Hold on again please."

Chief Kent listened to everyone's report. "We do not know how he got to Richmond Hill. We will check all taxi services and bus terminals. Oh, and Chief, his mom said he changed his clothes. He is wearing all black including his tennis shoes. One more thing, he is carrying five hundred thousand dollars on him"

"Smart kid," said Chief Benson.

"Yeah, I hope it does not get him killed," said Chief Kent. "He and Daviel want to be detectives. Call if you find him."

"Will do. I will get this information out to all my officers. Bye."

"What can we do?" asked Mrs. Scott. "Now, Daviel and Hal are both missing."

"Hold on a minute ma'am." Talking to the dispatcher he gave him Hal's description and said, "Check the bus station and all taxi services. The kid has over an hour head start so he probably is already in Richmond Hill. Chief Benson is looking for him."

***

Quietly Hal entered the mansion. Being Daviel's best friend and brother had its advantages. He went to Daviel's bedroom, opened the safe, took out the money, and left before anyone knew he was there. Next, he went to his house and changed into all black. Smiling to himself he thought, *It sure is a good thing that Daviel and I have played so many secret agent games. I'll find Daviel if it is the last thing I do!*

I cannot take any of our cars. Chief Kent will put out an APB on them as soon as they realize I am gone. I hope I am long gone before they realize it. Mom is going to kill me, he thought.

Surely, they will check the bus terminal and all taxi stands. How can I get to Richmond Hill without leaving a trail? I know!

Hal went over to Alex's house. Alex had a large motorcycle that would easily carry him and Daviel when he found him. It was late but Hal managed to get Alex to open his bedroom window by tapping on it.

"Hal, what are you doing? Have you heard any-thing about Daviel?"

"Will you keep a secret?" asked Hal. "I am going after Daviel, will you help me?"

"Of course, to both questions." replied Alex. "Do you want me to come with you?"

"No! But, thanks. I need to borrow your motorcycle. We have a tip as to where Daviel might be."

"Where's that?" questioned Alex.

"The less you know the less trouble you will get into. Can I use your bike or not? I'm in a hurry!"

"Sure," said Alex as he left his bedroom window. It was a good thing that his bedroom was on the bottom floor and at the back of the house. He quietly opened the garage door and gave Hal the keys and his helmet.

"Thanks, my friend. I will return your bike as soon as I can. Pray for me," said Hal as he pushed the motorcycle to the street and down a ways before starting her up.

Alex would have liked to go with Hal to rescue Daviel but secretly he was glad that Hal said no. He had no interest in being a detective. Alex returned to his house, said a prayer, and went back to sleep.

Hal started the motorcycle and was on his way. It took him an hour to reach Richmond Hill. It was midnight when he got there. Now what do I do? He thought. I'm sure the police have searched everywhere for the kidnappers. If I were a kidnapper where would I hide? The possibilities were endless.

Hal rode the motorcycle slowly around the outskirts of Richmond Hill. Not finding anything he decided to look for some side roads and rode down several of them. He rode five miles down each and turned around. He was getting discouraged.

Now is not the time to be discouraged, he thought. *Daviel is here somewhere and he is depending on me to find him.*

Hal decided to check the other side of town. As he was riding down a dirt road, he saw an abandoned old shack. He could not see any lights but decided that he should check it out.

Hal thought for a while and decided to hide the motorcycle in the woods. He and Daviel would have to escape the kidnappers and run to the bike if he was there.

Hal hid the bike so that it could not be seen and started to head back to the road when he heard a car coming.

What would a car be doing out here, he wondered, *unless it is the police looking for me,* he thought as he ducked under cover.

The car was coming up the dirt road towards Richmond Hill without using its headlights. When the car passed Hal recognized Raul. *So,* he thought excitedly, *I am on the right track and with only one *kidnapper it will be easier to rescue Daviel. Thank you Lord and please help me,* he prayed.

Hal crept up to the shack. At the back of the house he could see a small stream of light through the covered window. He looked inside through a small knot hole and saw Daviel tied to the bed and Miguel smoking a cigar.

"Tomorrow kid may just be your last day to live. If that old man of yours don't pay, Raul will probably kill you."

"I'm sure you will shed a few tears for me. Do I not even get a last meal?" Daviel jested.

Laughing, Miguel left his chair and walked over to the boy. "You have a lot of spunk kid. I really wish I could let you go but you know how it is."

Hal was trying to decide how he could let Daviel know he was there. The bed that Daviel was on was on an outside wall so he walked around the house and lightly tapped on the wall. He hoped that only Daviel would be able to hear him and that Miguel couldn't. It was good that Daviel had them both learn Morse Code. Quietly he tapped out "Get Miguel to come outside."

Daviel kicked the wall which made Miguel jump. "What's the problem kid?" asked Miguel.

"I need to use the bathroom before I go to sleep," Daviel said.

"Oh, all right." Miguel lifted Daviel to his feet and carried him into the woods. Daviel couldn't run because his feet were tied and his hands were tied behind his back. He really did need to go to the bathroom.

"Don't try anything funny kid our else!" declared Miguel.

While Miguel started to untie Daviel's hands Hal snuck up behind him and clobbered him over the head with a small log. Miguel went out like a light.

"How did you get here? How did you find me?" asked an ecstatic Daviel.

"There is no time for questions. We must hurry before Raul gets back."

Hal grabbed Miguel's knife and cut Daviel loose. While Daviel massaged his wrists and ankles Hal tied Miguel up and drug him into the woods. He quickly entered the house and grabbed a pillow case that was lying on the floor. He stuffed part of it in Miguel's mouth and tied the rest around Miguel's head. After hiding the body as best he could he spread dried leaves around to cover up the marks dragging the body had left. Satisfied he went over to Daviel.

"He won't be calling out for help with that gag," said Hal. "Can you walk little brother? I have a motorcycle hid out in the woods."

Daviel took a step and pain shot through his legs. He moaned and fell to the ground. Hal started massaging his legs which caused Daviel more pain. Before Daviel was ready Raul came back.

"I have to get you deeper into the woods before Raul sees us."

Hal grabbed Daviel under his arms and helped him into the woods. Daviel tried to help as much as he could but it was precious little help.

While the boys were making their escape, Raul entered the cabin and found it empty. He figured that Daviel needed to go to the bathroom again and waited. After a few minutes he started getting worried and stepped outside and softly called, "Miguel, Miguel where are you?"

He thought, *You had better not be pulling a double cross Miguel or when I find you it will be curtains for you!*

Chapter 14
THE CHASE

Hal continued to half drag Daviel deeper into the woods. Slowly the feeling in Daviel's legs was returning to normal.

"I am okay Hal, let me walk," said Daviel. "It will not take Raul long to find Miguel and we have to hurry. Where is the motorcycle?"

"It is at the entrance to the dirt road. We will have to circle around."

As the two boys started for the motorbike, they heard Miguel thrashing in the woods. They saw Raul cautiously walk up to him. Quickly Raul removed the gag.

"What happened to you and where is Daviel?"

"I don't know where Daviel is moron. Someone hit me on the back of the head and out I went. He is probably miles from here by now!" lamented Miguel.

They heard Miguel's loud comment and smiled at each other. "Let's get out of here," Hal said.

It was slow going. Although Daviel was feeling better every second he still had not used his legs for four days and with the lack of food was somewhat wobbly on his feet.

Both boys were careful not to step on any twigs. However, when they were half way to the motorcycle the inevitable happened. Daviel stepped on a twig which broke with a loud noise.

"It came from over there," said Raul as he pulled out his pistol. Watching the woods, he saw a flash of white from Daviel's t-shirt and fired.

Why didn't I think to bring Daviel some black clothes, thought Hal as he pulled Daviel to the ground?

Another shot rang out and struck a tree beside the boys. Hal pulled out his dad's thirty-eight and fired back.

Daviel was shocked. "Where did you get that!" he exclaimed.

"It is dad's. If we get home alive, I will be grounded for a month if not the rest of my life!"

Daviel quietly laughed. Hal probably was right and he realized just how much his best friend had risked to come after him.

"Can you see them" asked Hal.

"No, can you," replied Daviel.

"No, wait, I see them now. They are separating. Miguel is going deeper into the woods and trying get around behind us. I will wait for a clear shot and hope for the best," said Hal.

Hal watched Raul and Miguel. He saw Miguel enter a clearing and fired. He heard Miguel yell and drop to the ground.

"Did you kill him," asked Daviel.

"I hope not. You know that I have never fired a gun in my life.   Only the good Lord knows where I hit him."

The boys saw Raul running towards his friend and they took off running for the motorcycle. Shortly they heard a scream.

"You killed him! I am going to kill you both!" yelled Raul.

Abandoning all caution, the boys ran for their lives. Raul chased after them and fired several times coming close to hitting the boys. Hal fired back at Raul as he ran. He never came close but the shots made Raul be more careful.

The boys reached the entrance to the road and Daviel yelled, "Where is the bike?"

"It is right over there," he said pointing. "You get the thing started and I will hold off your friend."

Hal was feeling better about their chance of escaping. A bullet whistling past his ear took care of that.

Daviel got the motorcycle started and Hal jumped on. He shot behind him again and almost shot Raul.

I have to get out of here before the police come, thought Raul. He headed back for the car. There was nothing that he could do for Miguel. The bullet struck him in the head and his friend was bleeding. Miguel was dead and he would make those brats pay!

Daviel drove straight to police headquarters and he and Hal told their stories.

"Raul said that Miguel was dead. Raul is probably trying to escape in a 2002 maroon Chrysler LeBaron with a half leather light brown top. I never saw the license plate."

"We just received calls about some shots being fired. Where were you boys?"

"We have no idea," said Hal. "I found Daviel in an old abandoned shack west of town."

"That is where the shots were reported to be coming from," said the officer.

The officer sent two squad cars to the area. One was to look for Raul and the other was to bring in the body of Miguel. Next, he called the chief who promised to come immediately.

"May I call my parents and let them know that I am all right?" asked Daviel.

"Certainly, and tell them you are being incarcerated for carrying a concealed weapon without a permit," said the officer.

"I do not have a concealed weapon officer!"

"No, but your friend does, and you are with him so that makes you an accessory to the crime."

Daviel called his parents. He explained that Hal had rescued him, the chase, the killing of Miguel, and that they were being incarcerated for carrying a concealed weapon without a permit.

The judge said that he, mom, and Hal's parents would leave for Richmond Hill immediately, told Daviel that he loved him, and would see him soon.

Daviel and Hal were arrested and locked up. When the officer searched Hal, he found the five hundred thousand dollars on him.

"What's this?" asked the officer.

"It is five hundred thousand dollars," replied Chief Benson.

"Chief!" exclaimed the officer. "I was just locking these two up for carrying a concealed weapon without a permit," the officer explained.

"Fine, but first put the money in the safe. I want to talk to these boys."

Daviel and Hal followed the chief to his office. While they were there, they overheard one of the patrol cars say that they had a dazed Miguel. The bullet only grazed his head and knocked him out. He would bring him in.

The other patrol car called and reported that the LeBaron had been wrecked. More men would be needed to search for Raul. Chief Benson dispatched ten men to help with the search.

"Don't worry boys. He will not escape," said the chief with confidence.

"Now suppose you boys tell me the whole story from the beginning. Daviel , why don't you go first. Hal, I pretty much know most of yours."

Hal blushed and couldn't look the chief in the eye.

While Daviel was telling his story starting with being kidnapped an officer entered with Miguel. The chief and the boys left his office to watch him being booked.

Miguel looked at the boys and said, "You shot me, I can't believe you shot me in the head!"

"Well, you were trying to kill us," said Daviel.

Hal said, "I was aiming for your legs!"

"You missed," said the chief with a grin.

The boys were in the chief's office when their parents walked in. The two boys were surrounded and smothered in hugs. Miguel heard the commotion from his cell. He wondered if Raul had escaped. He realized that Raul thought he was dead and would not have left him otherwise. He thought, I should have dumped the moron years ago!

Again, Daviel told his story. Mrs. McKnight was furious for the way they had treated her son and wanted to give Miguel a piece of her mind but the judge got her settled down.

Hal was a hero but he knew his parents were not happy with him for taking the pistol. "I know that I am in trouble for taking dad's pistol but I'm not sorry I did it. If I didn't have the pistol we would have been killed."

"We will talk about that later son," said his dad. "If you hadn't taken off and let the police do their job you would not be in so much trouble now. You have to be less impetuous."

"Yes sir," said Hal.

Daviel put his arm around his brother, "I do not know about anyone else but I am glad you came brother. I haven't eaten much in days, how about a pizza. Hal's buying," he joked, "he has plenty of money, that is if the police will let us use it."

Everyone laughed except Hal. He knew that he was in big trouble with his parents.

CHAPTER 15
THE VICTORY CELEBRATION

Hal was in trouble but he also was a celebrity. The boys did not have to stay in jail. They were released to the custody of their parents and were even allowed to sleep in the same hotel room. News quickly spread about Daviel's rescue and the police had to keep the reporters at bay.

Raul's body was found the next day. He had sustained some serious injuries from the crash and bled to death in the woods while trying to escape. Justice had been served.

Hal and Daviel rode Alex's motorcycle back to Savannah the next day. Hal's parents followed them and after returning the bike, they headed for the island. The mainland boat dock was surrounded by reporters so they went to the marina and rented a boat thus escaping the press for a while.

Police Chief Kent came to the island and after hearing the whole story congratulated Hal on a job well done. Hal was a hero in Daviel's eyes and he could not sing his praises enough.

The press was frustrated because no one would comment on the kidnapping. They did go to the jail and interview Miguel who gladly told his story — for a price.

Daviel knew that he would not get any relief from the press unless he held a news conference which his father scheduled for the next day. Today he just wanted to relax in his beautiful home with Hal and stare at his beautiful daggers.

While the boys were silently thinking their own thoughts, their parents walked in.

Uh oh, thought Hal as he sat up.

"Are you boys enjoying yourselves?" asked Mr. Scott.

"Um, yes sir," replied Hal.

Daviel knew that Hal was in trouble and wanted to help him but did not know what to do. Hal was his hero and he did not take lightly what he had done. Hal had put his own life in danger to save his.

"We need to talk," said Mr. Scott.

Daviel interrupted, "Sir, I know that Hal should not have taken your pistol but if he had not, we would be dead."

"Yes Daviel, I know that, but if Hal had not taken off like he did you both would not have been shot at," replied Hal's dad.

"Yes sir, that is true, but if Hal had not come to rescue me Raul would have killed me for not getting the ransom money."

"Um, Daviel, I guess I need to tell you. I was going to pay the ransom," said the judge.

"You were?" asked a surprised Daviel. "But I thought we had an agreement."

"We did, but I never promised I would not pay it."

Daviel looked at his dad.

"You are more precious to us than all the money in the world dear," said his mother.

"I know that mom, and you two are more precious to me than anything and so is Hal. If he had been kidnapped, I would have gone after him. He is my hero. I do not want to see him punished for saving my life. I would do the same for him no matter the risk."

"Daviel, we understand the special bond that the two of you have and Hal's mother and I are very proud of you both, but what Hal did was wrong. You do understand that, right?"

"I guess so, but could the punishment start after the celebration dinner and does this mean that we cannot be friends?"

"We have not decided on a punishment yet and have decided to enlist the help of you boys." Turning to his son he said, "Hal, your mom and I are very proud of you. You risked your life to prove your love for Daviel and for that we are proud. You are a hero. The police may have found Daviel eventually but they had searched for him twice without success. Of course, you knew that."

Looking at his wife he said, "Your mom and I should have guessed what you would do and stopped you but we were so excited to know that Daviel was somewhere in Richmond Hill that we did not think through what that information would mean to you. Isn't that right dear?"

Hal's mom nodded her head in agreement.

"Mrs. McKnight and I are very grateful to you Hal and cannot thank you enough for what you did."

"I–I accused you of not loving Daviel," said a shamefaced boy.

"That was your emotions Hal. I understand and you have been forgiven so it is forgotten. We may have underestimated your love for Daviel though. None of us expected you to do what you did. You showed intelligence in changing your clothes and taking the pistol."

"Really!"

"Yes really," said Hal's dad. "That does not mean you won't be punished though and Daviel we are thrilled with your friendship with Hal and want to see that friendship continue to grow."

Daviel looked relieved. He was not going to lose his best friend.

"What do you boys think would be a fitting pun-ishment for Hal's taking the gun?" asked Mr. Scott.

Hal and Daviel had talked about it. They both knew that Hal should not have taken his father's gun. Hal looked at his dad and said, "Daviel and I have talked about it and we agree that whatever punishment you give me we will accept it even if it meant ending our friendship." Hal looked at Daviel for agreement.

"That is what we agreed to. You are Hal's parents; I am simply an adopted brother and where it would break my heart to lose Hal's friendship, I will accept whatever punishment you feel is fair. However, no matter what, Hal will always be my brother and I will always love him."

"Mrs. Scott and I know that Daviel, and we have no intention of not allowing Hal to see you. You are both very godly young men and you both demonstrate maturity beyond your years,"

"But," said Daviel. He was not sure if they were winning or losing!

Before he could say more, Hal's dad said, "Hal, your mom and I have decided that you will be put on restriction for one month. After the celebration dinner you will go to school and return to the house. You will be confined to the house. You may not call anyone or talk to anyone outside of school and church during your month probation. Also, you may not date Pam for one month. You may not drive your car to school or church. We are proud of you but taking my pistol could have had serious consequences and your mom and I feel that discipline is necessary. Any questions?"

"No sir, except you did say that this would start after the celebration dinner, right?"

"Yes, I did. After Friday night's dinner you, young man, are on strict detention."

"Yes sir."

"Do either of you have any comments?" asked the judge.

"No sir, we agreed to abide by whatever decision Hal's parents decided was best for Hal." Walking over to Hal, Daviel gave him a hug and said, "Thank You! I will see you at the celebration dinner. I love you," and went to his room.

One month was not too long and besides he would at least see Hal at school and church. The punishment could have been much, much worse.

There was a knock at Daviel's door as he lay on his bed. "Come in," he called.

His father walked in and sat on the bed beside the boy. "Are you okay?" he asked.

"Yes sir, but I am not sure that I understand. Oh, Hal and I will abide by his parent's decision even if they had ended our friendship. Nothing will ever change the way we feel about each other." Sitting up he said, "Dad, Hal saved my life. I think that Raul would have killed me even if he had received the ransom. Miguel showed some compassion but Raul was happy only when he was hurting me."

"You are probably right, Raul probably would have killed you, but son, you and Hal are only boys. Hal should have left finding you up to the police. I think the Lord would have helped them find you."

"Yes sir, but the Lord did help Hal. He let Hal see Raul leave and know where I was. Dad, Raul went to town every night and the police never spotted him. I know taking the pistol was wrong as well as illegal but I am glad that he did. I cannot help it; he saved my life."

"I too am glad but remember son never do wrong to do right."

"Yes, sir I know. Anyway, we will have a month to ponder over it and maybe in that time the Lord will help us to understand how wrong it really was to take the pistol."

"I will pray that He will. Good night son."

"Good night Dad."

At the news conference Daviel explained how he was kidnapped and the connection to his stolen daggers. He explained how he was tied up and about the two kidnappers and their differences. Next, he explained about the agreement between he and his dad to never pay a ransom for him.

When he was through Hal explained his part in the rescue. Everyone said he was a hero and Daviel agreed.

One news reporter asked the judge if he would have paid the ransom. The judge answered, "I guess we will never know!"

Friday night the celebration dinner was a giant success. Hal was very embarrassed at being hailed as a hero. Pam and Rita were both there and the boys explained about Hal's restriction and since they had planned to only double date Daviel and Rita would wait for Hal's restriction to end. After receiving Pam's permission and Hal's parent's permission Rita gave Hal a kiss on his check in front of everyone and told him thank you for saving Daviel's life. Hal blushed but not for the last time.

Daviel stood to his feet and said, "I propose a toast."

Everyone stood to their feet and grabbed their crystal goblets filled with sparkling grape juice.

"To Hal, my hero, best friend, and big brother. I love you brother," said Daviel raising his glass to a blushing Hal.

Sneak Peek

THE MYSTERY OF THE JEWELED STATUE

Daviel (Dah–V–El) and Hal solved the mystery of the stolen daggers in book two. Now it was time for school to begin. Both boys turned sixteen last summer, Hal on July 18th and Daviel on July 21st. Hal was three days older than his best friend and he did not let Daviel forget it.

Today was the first day of school. They would both be Juniors at their Christian school.   Being a small school, they had the same classes along with their girls, Rita and Pam. Rita is Daviel's girl and Pam is Hals.

Daviel is a multi-millionaire. He lives on an island off the Savannah coast. His best friend, since the eighth grade, is Hal. They are always together. Hal lives with his mom and dad on the Savannah coast. In fact, Hal can see Daviel's island from his bedroom window. The two boys are like brothers and they love to solve mysteries. They plan to attend a detective school after they graduate. Right now, they are taking Karate classes and studying The Hardy Boys Detective Handbook to learn about crime detection.

Daviel awoke to a good breakfast. His Aunt Chris was an excellent cook and she believed that a boy needed a good breakfast before going to school. After breakfast, Daviel went to Hal's house. He was now encouraging his best friend to get ready more quickly as he did not want to be late his first day of school.

"Are you ready for another year?" asked Daviel.

"No, not really. I wish that I were as smart as you. Then I would not have to spend so much time studying. I hope I can keep up my grades and do karate too. After our last case, The Mystery of the Stolen Daggers, I want karate lessons. Dad said that I could have them only if I keep my grades up."

"What are you worried about. You have never made lower than a B and besides I will help you if you run into any trouble," encouraged Daviel.

"Thanks, but I also want some time with Pam. I really like her and you know that mom and dad will not allow any dating if I make a C on my report card. Besides, eleventh grade is harder than tenth. What if I cannot do everything? What if —"

"When did you become such a worry wart?" asked Daviel. "Oh, I get it. You are not really worried about Karate classes; you are worried about not being able to go on any dates with Pam. That should not be a problem. You cannot date for a month anyway so, big brother, you can use this month to study really hard and make those good grades."

Hal was on a month restriction for taking his dad's thirty-eight caliber pistol to rescue Daviel from his kidnappers.

Hal gave his friend a smile. "I do want Karate lessons but I want to have dates more and you are right, I have to wait a month before I can start dating."

"I promise, you are worrying about nothing, but if you cannot do the Karate lessons and date, I guess you will have to give up dating," teased Daviel.

"What!" exclaimed Hal. "No way! I'll give up Karate lessons first." He started to go on but Daviel stopped him.

"If you cannot keep up your grades, though I do not know why you couldn't because you are very intelligent, you may stop the Karate classes. Okay?"

"Okay," agreed Hal.

They made it to school just in the nick of time. They entered their homeroom class as the late bell rang.

"We have to do better tomorrow," Daviel whispered. "You know brother that I like time to relax before starting class."

"Good morning class. My name is Mrs. Spenaker. I will be your homeroom teacher and English teacher. Please answer here as I call out your names. Also, as I call out your names, please take the seats up front and fill them in towards the back of the room. That will help me to learn your names. Amberstcrombie, Daviel."

"Here ma'am," responded Daviel as he took the front row seat. Since the class was small Hal got the seat right behind him. Rita and Pam got to sit next to each other as their names were Jenkins and Jones.

The first day of classes went well. Daviel and Hal drove the girls to their homes. After saying goodbye, they went to Hal's house to talk about their homework.

"Man, I thought that I was going to have a heart attack when Mrs. Spenaker started talking about the ten-page term paper that we have to write," Hal said.

"You have written term papers before. What is the problem?"

"Well, yeah, but she wants foot notes and references and she said that these would have to be written like college term papers."

"True," said Daviel, "but our English book tells us exactly what to do. It will just take a little more time that is all."

"Time!" exclaimed Hal, "is something that I don't have. Can't I quit Karate before we start classes next week?"

"NO!" Daviel practically shouted. "I think that having a girl friend is not good for you. You are a basket case and it is only the first day of school. We will handle any problems as they come. Besides, you can get started on your term paper this month since you cannot date until next month. That will give you plenty of time!"

The next two weeks were hard for the boys. The teachers explained that colleges took this year's grades more serious than the other years. Colleges expect students to settle down by eleventh grade. This made Hal even more nervous. So far, he had made all A's on his exams but could he keep it up.

"Tomorrow you will have an English grammar test. It will cover pages twelve through twenty-six in your books. This is a hard test and I would advise some serious study time," said Mrs. Spenaker.

After class Rita suggested that they all come to her house to study. Daviel was excited by the idea and since Pam would be there too Hal seconded the idea.

"Great!" exclaimed Hal. "Daviel and I will take you home and then come back with pizzas around five thirty, ok. That is if my parents will let me off restriction."

"Sounds good to me," Pam said, "how does it sound to you Rita?"

"That will be fine. It will give us some time to clean the den and I have a few other chores that I need to do."

The boys went home and explained their plans to their families. Hal's dad cautioned Hal to study and not just have fun. He then reminded him that if his grades fell, he would not be able to date.

Hal told Daviel on the way to school the next day, "I sure am glad that we studied last night. I have to make a good grade on this test."

"You will. We studied hard and you answered all the questions correctly that we asked you, so stop worrying. What happened to my happy go lucky brother?" Daviel asked

Hal ignored the question because he did not know the answer. After taking his father's pistol to rescue Daviel a few weeks ago and then being put on restriction, something happened to him. After school the four young people met.

"How do you think you boys did?" asked Rita. "Pam and I feel that we did well."

"I am sure that I made an A," declared Daviel.

"You always make an A," laughed Pam as she turned to Hal. "How about you?"

"I know that I passed but I had some problems remembering some of the answers. I hope I at least made a B."

Two days later the grades were posted on the board.

"You look," said Hal, "I can't"

"Ok," laughed Daviel as he went to the board and wrote down theirs and the girl's grades."

"Well," asked Hal. "Did I pass?"

"You made a ninety-three."

"Whoopee!!" shouted Hal. His class mates turned and smiled at him.

"I take it you passed," said a voice behind him.

Turning, he saw Pam and Rita. Daviel told the two of them their grades and they were happy with them.

"How did you do?" asked Hal.

"Oh, I passed," answered Daviel.

He refused to tell them his grade. They always expected him to make a hundred and they often teased him about it.

"Come on," said Rita. "What grade did you get? Tell us or we will go look at the board."

Daviel remained silent until the girls started heading for the board.

"Ok, ok, I made a hundred."

The two girls looked at each other and laughed. "What else!" they exclaimed.

"I cannot help it if the Lord made me smart. You would not want me to fail, would you?"

Everyone in the class laughed at the thought of Daviel failing. He blushed.

The month passed and then another. All four of them continued to make good grades. It was time for Daviel and Hal to earn their yellow belts in Karate. It normally took six months to move from a white belt to a yellow belt but both boys excelled at karate and were able to try to advance in three months. Both boys, who normally did not like physical exercise, really were enjoying the Karate lessons, especially Hal. He was a little better than Daviel and he rejoiced that he could beat Daviel at something.

Their families came to watch them take their test. Both boys had different opponents than each other and they were glad for this. Hal easily conquered his opponent but Daviel lost his match though he still got his yellow belt. Actually, losing was good for him. Even though he never bragged about his grades or how smart he was it was good that he did not excel at everything or else he might become prideful. After class everyone congratulated the two boys.

"Great match Hal," said his dad as he patted him on the back. "Your mom and I are very proud of you."

"Great job son," said the Judge as he hugged Daviel.

He did not make excuses for Daviel's loss. He knew the boy had done his best and that was all he expected from him. Daviel loved the judge and Mrs. McKnight as if they were his own parents instead of just his legal guardians.

"Thanks dad," he said and then turned to congratulate Hal.

"Awesome job Hal."

"You too."

Nothing was said about Hal winning and Daviel losing until Daviel mentioned it at the restaurant.

"I want to say thank you to all of you who never said that I lost my match, especially you," he said turning to Hal. "I really appreciate it."

"What would I say?" asked Hal. "We are both yellow belts."

Daviel smiled at his best friend. Then he laughed. Everyone looked at him waiting for an explanation. "You are terrific Hal. You know good and well that you are better than I am at Karate. If we had ten matches you would win seven or eight of them. You —"

"Stop," interrupted Hal, "you are embarrassing me. Besides, you are better than I at everything else, so, I am glad that I can beat you at something."

"You beat me at a lot of things," declared Daviel.

"Name one," said Hal.

Before Daviel could start the judge interrupted. "Boys, this is a celebration and you can save that discussion for a later time. Both of you are special in your own ways and we are all proud of you for who you are. Right?"

"Right!" everyone agreed.

The rest of the evening passed quietly.

Also by Daniel S. Wyckoff, Sr.

THE LAND OF GARUMPH

Daniel and Scott are taken by spaceship to a fantastic world where animals talk! Here they discover they are chosen to protect the kingdom of Garumph from the wicked Natas. A difficult journey, they set off to find the key to saving the kingdom before the evil shadow covers the entire land.

Along the way they learn important life lessons, such as: Is God Everywhere? Looks are Deceiving, and True Friendship. Perfect for 7-12 year olds searching for their place in the world and longing for a little adventure.

This book is rated G

Collect all ***The Amazing Master Daviel Amberst-crombie* series**

The Mystery of Crescent Hook Island
The Mystery of the Stolen Daggers
The Mystery of the Jeweled Statue

These books are rated PG for mild violence

The Adventures Contiune...

If you enjoyed *The Amazing Master Daviel Amberstcrombie* series, you may also enjoy this mystery novel by Brianna C. Daring Wyckoff

Taken by Mistake

Jesse Target lives a double life. To the common citizen he's an ordinary American teenager. To a select few he's Jesse Best—top class detective and undercover agent. His life has been anything but normal, and it only gets more interesting when a chance meeting puts him face to face with a millionaire's son who looks exactly like him.

Unraveling the mystery that surrounds his look-alike is only part of Jesse's caseload. Just as things begin to settle down with Philip Taylor, Jesse is called to go undercover to discover who is pillaging a family estate in Nevada. How is he supposed to explain his sudden disappearance to his new best friend without exposing his true, but secret, identity?

Life seldom gives downtime, and Jesse isn't allowed any. His plane has hardly landed when he receives the terrible news that Philip has gone missing. He's vanished without a trace and Jesse can't help but wonder: Is it his fault?

This book is rated PG for mild violence

Also by Brianna C. Daring Wyckoff

Stormology
Gathering Storm

Javen Andrews only survives if he maintains his in-visibility.

Brought up in a family intent on hurting him, Javen does his best to avoid contact. But how can he stay in the shadows when someone else is at risk? When his presence is discovered, his father seizes the opportu-nity to use him for his own devices.

Kidnapped from the ocean, the feisty young mermaid doesn't need anyone, She can get herslef back home.

She certainly has no use for a worthless boy who can't even look his family in the eye—unless she can use him for her own gain.

A puppet. A pawn. But what if Javen is meant to be something more?

This book is rated PG-13 due to scenes of emotional and physical abuse.

And for your littlest adventurers, check out this children's book by Norene Wyckoff

The Adventures of Henry the Helicopter
Henry the Helicopter and the Slurpy Swamp

Henry isn't your average helicopter. He's a rescue helicopter with a peculiar hobby—jumping on his trampoline! When a distressed mother calls, begging him to find her two missing children, Henry sets off for the Slurpy Swamp praying to find them before something else does.

This book is rated G

www.ingramcontent.com/pod-product-compliance
Lightning Source LLC
Chambersburg PA
CBHW070952180726
48291CB00004B/1255